The Pearl-fishers

Other titles by Robin Jenkins

Dust on the Paw
Leila
Love is a Fervent Fire
Lunderston Tales
Matthew & Sheila
The Missionaries
Poverty Castle
Sardana Dancers
Some Kind of Grace
The Thistle and the Grail
A Very Scotch Affair
Willie Hogg

ROBIN JENKINS

The Pearl-fishers

First published in Great Britain in 2007 by Polygon,
an imprint of Birlinn Ltd

West Newington House
10 Newington Road
Edinburgh
EH9 1QS

9 8 7 6 5 4

www.birlinn.co.uk

ISBN 978 1 84697 006 1

British Library Cataloguing-in-Publication Data
A catalogue record for this book is available on request from the
British Library

The publisher acknowledges subsidy from

Scottish
Arts Council
LOTTERY FUNDED

towards the publication of this volume

Typeset in Janson Text by Palimpsest Book Production Ltd,
Grangemouth, Stirlingshire
Printed in Great Britain by Clays Ltd, St Ives plc

Introduction

The manuscript of *The Pearl-fishers* was found in a drawer after Robin Jenkins' death by his daughter. It had no title, and it was not clear whether this was a work he had intended for publication, or if he had put it aside because he was not happy with it. Three other versions of this novel are stored in the National Library of Scotland among the rest of the papers he bequeathed to the library, which arrived in a suitcase shortly after he died in 2005. One is the opening chapters of a very early draft, written in a spiral-bound notebook in Jenkins' tiny hand-writing. In this embryonic, untitled version, there are as many crossings out and alterations as there are untouched sentences, the pages a succession of inky matchstick words and scored-through lines whose meaning only becomes clear when one starts to decipher the miniscule print. The notebook is splattered with tea.

The two other versions are typescripts, bearing the title *The Tinker Girl*. One of them appears to be identical to the copy published here as *The Pearl-fishers* and must be, one assumes, a copy of the manuscript found in the drawer. The new title embraces the whole family at the centre of the story, a group of five weary travellers who make their living from the jewels to be found in Scottish freshwater mussels. The party comprises a dying grandfather, his middle-aged daughter and her three children, two of whom are young, and one, Effie Williamson, who is nineteen.

The original, politically incorrect title, *The Tinker Girl*, which focuses on Effie alone, would have been no mistake or slip on Jenkins' part. As he makes clear from the outset of the novel, the word tinker was an insult, freighted with centuries of suspicion and dislike on the part of those seemingly respectable citizens who mistrusted the travelling people as filthy, thieving, and possibly worse. Along with its overtones of ostracism and prejudice, however, that early title also evokes the almost fairy-tale quality of the story that follows, with its ancient resonances of outcasts trying to make their way in a world hostile to those who are unconventional, or unattractively poor. There is something fable-like about Effie, too, so out of kilter with the rest of her family that she might almost be a creature from another element or world, a selkie, sprite, or the heroine of a Border Ballad rather than a twentieth-century novel.

Jenkins, however, was not a fanciful novelist. For all his imaginative verve, his eye was firmly fixed on the moral universe rather than on any invisible faerie kingdom. Born in the village of Flemington, near Cambuslang in Lanarkshire in 1912, he was brought up by his mother after his father died when he was seven. He was a school-teacher by profession, and did not become a novelist until he was nearly forty, when he published *So Gaily Sings the Lark* in 1951. Thereafter, however, he made up for his late start by producing a novel every couple of years from a seemingly fathomless store of ideas. A widely travelled man, he taught in Afghanistan, Spain and Borneo, using these locations for some of his work, although he set more of his books in Scotland than abroad.

In an output of around thirty books, he attracted acclaim

for many of his novels, but two were notable triumphs: the masterly tragedy *The Cone-gatherers* (1955), about a conscientious objector and his hunchbacked brother, who come into conflict with an estate gamekeeper; and the complex first-person account, *Fergus Lamont* (1979), his portrait of a sardonic poet, born in the slums of Glasgow, who tries to distance himself from his rough upbringing, yet can never settle in his new-found aristocratic milieu.

One of the intriguing aspects of *The Pearl-fishers* is that it shares the same setting – the Ardmore forest in Argyllshire – as Jenkins used in *The Cone-gatherers*, as well as in his first novel, and takes place only a few years after those unhappy events. This seemingly edenic backdrop offers Jenkins' characters space for spiritual clarity, a timeless, unworldly environment where the essentials of life can be calmly examined. In the case of *The Pearl-fishers*, those essentials include an almost holy degree of goodness, and a young woman's torment on discovering love, but mistrusting not only the motives of the man offering it, but what may become of her – psychologically as well as materially – if she succumbs to her desires.

The story is told largely from the perspective of the beautiful and courageous Effie, who has brought her family by horse and cart over two hundred miles from Sutherland to Argyll, so her terminally ill grandfather can die and be buried near his own people. Her counterpart in the tale is Gavin Hamilton, already known to Jenkins' readers as hero of his deeply contemplative novel *A Would-be Saint*. *The Pearl-fishers* is thus doubly interesting, introducing the admirable Effie, but also continuing the story of a man with some claim to be the most likeable, if stubborn, of Jenkins' creations.

In this new novel, Hamilton is lightly sketched, perhaps too lightly for those who have not previously encountered him. As the earliest handwritten copy of the book shows, Jenkins initially described him at some length, as one of the foresters who 'spoke least and smiled most'; later he edited back his introduction to this uncompromisingly, almost indecently humane man removing, among others, a sarcastic reference to him as 'a would-be saint' and the fact that he gave part of his pay to a charity for the poor.

When we meet Hamilton and Effie, in the years immediately following the Second World War, Hamilton is a forester in Ardmore forest, where he had worked as a conscientious objector. In *A Would-be Saint*, Jenkins follows Hamilton's life, from boyhood in a Lanarkshire mining town, when his father is killed in the First World War. From a very young age, Hamilton showed himself to be different from other children, hating to see anyone hurt or bullied. A clever boy, who would have gone to university had his mother not died, he was also such a good footballer that he might have been signed for clubs such as Hearts or Queen's Park.

Widely liked, despite being taunted as a Creeping Jesus for his heart-on-the-sleeve Christianity, he nevertheless had few real friends. When the Second World War broke out, he became a pacifist and, like other 'conchies' in Jenkins' fiction, ended up in Ardmore forest. This was where his story ended, shortly after the end of the war. Jenkins, however, clearly wanted to know what turn his life next took.

As he intimates in the opening chapters, Hamilton is now planning to become a Church of Scotland minister, and is going to university in the autumn. Already his godly otherness is making some people uncomfortable. He unsettles the foresters' wives: 'Though it was in their nature to be hospitable they were always relieved when he left. It was as if they had done something wrong – although they had absolutely no idea what it was – and Hamilton felt it his duty to help them find forgiveness.' As Jenkins later writes, 'Those who carefully measured their own charity thought he had a damned cheek trying to show himself more Christian than anyone else.' Therein lies one of the author's most vexed questions: the dilemma of how to live a charitably honourable life without implicitly or offensively denouncing others.

What he makes less clear in this novel than in *A Would-be Saint*, is that Hamilton is not a prig. He is simply – and complicatedly – a good man trying to live out his beliefs. The survival of decency and innocence or idealism in a corrupt world is a common Jenkins theme. It takes a dramatic turn in this novel when Hamilton takes the travelling family into his house. In *A Would-be Saint* he brought home a pregnant prostitute he had known at school, to the vulgar amusement of the town. The intervention of his outraged girlfriend, who paid the girl to leave, not only ended his engagement but cut short this experiment in compassion. Now he has another chance. Yet idealist as he is, even Hamilton knows that 'there was no virtue in being kind to people if in doing so you humiliated them'.

What he has not bargained on is falling in love with the girl. When, within a few days of meeting her, he asks her to marry him, he sets off a chain of complications, the simplest of which are the social implications of this unlikely union. Far more interesting and complex are the psychological and emotional consequences of such a marriage, all of which are seen from Effie's point of view.

With typical directness and earthy sensitivity, Jenkins imagines the inner life of a girl in her poverty-stricken and precarious position: 'Effie's own hopes of escaping her present way of life were almost extinguished. Who would come and rescue her? No one in the whole world.' But she is wrong. Here is a handsome young man, who unlike most other men she has known does not want simply to get her into bed, but appears to admire her and to want to care for her, and her young brother and sister. Among the many problems this declaration of love creates is a question of pride. As one of Hamilton's fellow foresters comments: 'He's probably thinking that this is the best opportunity he's ever had to show what a good Christian he is. She won't let herself be used in that way.' In *A Would-be Saint*, one girl's father advises her, 'Better an alcoholic for a husband than a would-be saint.' This novel could be read as Jenkins' attempt to address that throw-away remark. Thus a seemingly simple love story becomes fraught with ethical and emotional ramifications.

The Pearl-fishers could be seen as an account of what happens when a prayer is answered; of what to do or feel when someone, and something, is almost too good to be true. Though it is told in simple, pared-down style, with almost parable-like simplicity, there's a serious grittiness in this novel. Almost roughly at times, Jenkins addresses the harshness of life for a young woman like Effie, and for her less thoughtful mother's unplanned offspring. Unafraid to discuss sex, rape, and physical or mental brutality, he allows the suicide of Effie's grandmother to hover broodingly over the tale.

Written, one assumes, sometime after the publication of *A Would-be Saint* in 1978, *The Pearl-fishers* has many of Jenkins' usual ingredients: strongly drawn characters who combine a measure of decency with unthinking small-mindedness; a high degree of hypocrisy and moral cowardice among the so-called good and great; and throughout it all, a quest for a spiritually ethical way of life, the whole recounted in a compelling but uncompromisingly pastoral tone, with the author ministering to his readership like a preacher to his flock. The rather appealing period feel of the novel is perhaps a product of Jenkins' excessive economy of style. While on some levels it is a less sophisticated novel than many of his others, even so, it is a powerfully affecting and memorable tale.

Jenkins once wrote that: 'If it was to save itself from being used for evil purposes goodness needed its own kind of cunning and stubbornness.' *The Pearl-fishers* sees his hero Hamilton take that credo and begin to live by it. The tantalising question that hangs over this novel is, can he make it work?

Rosemary Goring
February 2007

One

EVERY SECOND Saturday, at midday, the men came out of the forest and gathered at the hut beside the road to collect their pay. If the weather was reasonably good, that's to say if it wasn't pouring, they would linger for a while before cycling off home, most of them in the direction of the little fishing village at the mouth of the sea loch, and one or two towards the remotenesses at its head, where their crofts were. Used to working in lonely places, often alone, they looked forward to those relaxed chats, enjoying one another's company, joking and laughing, mostly in Gaelic, enquiring after their respective families, discussing their work, mentioning sightings of otters, deer, pine martens and eagles, and making arrangements for the weekend.

One was noticeably different from the rest. An observer, asked to pick out from among the dozen or so the one who as a sideline took church services when the ministers were ill or on holiday, would without hesitation have pointed to Hamilton. Not just because of his black beard which, according to Deirdre McTeague, the forester's ten-year-old daughter, gave him a resemblance to Jesus feeding the five thousand as depicted in one of her Sunday school tracts. Even if he had been clean-shaven his remote inward gaze would have set him apart. Our observer if he himself was proficient in Gaelic must have noticed, if a story or joke was being told that needed a little profanity to give it point, that the raciest and most idiomatic Gaelic was used. This was so that Hamilton, whose Gaelic was not so fluent, wouldn't be able to follow it and therefore would not have to feel offended. His ambition was to be a minister of the Church of Scotland. His workmates didn't mind so long as he didn't try to practise his Christianity on them.

He was seldom invited to their homes. Their wives were never quite at ease in his company. When he visited them it was as the would-be minister and not as the workmate of their husbands. Though it was their nature to be hospitable they were always relieved when he left. It was as if they had done something wrong – although they had absolutely no idea what it was – and Hamilton felt it his duty to help them find forgiveness. They complained to their husbands, who laughed. 'That's just Gavin. What do you expect from a man that reads his Bible on the hill and once gave his whole pay packet to a tramp?'

What made it still more baffling was that the children, even the toddlers, seemed to have no difficulty in under-standing him. They even called him Uncle Gavin.

The two women who had known him best, Sheila McTeague, the forester's wife, and her friend Mary McGilp, a land-girl who had almost got engaged to him, had often discussed him. They had decided that his agonies of conscience during the war had left him in some way spiri-tually maimed. He had become incapable of showing love and perhaps of feeling it; except in the case of children.

Mary had gone back to Glasgow where she had married a man who had served on bomber planes, without damage to his mind or soul.

But if Hamilton was ever to become a successful minister

he would have to have a wife. Miss Fiona, the Kilcalmonell minister's sister, had offered herself, but she was at least ten years older and very plain, with no figure to speak of. That would hardly matter. They couldn't imagine her in bed with a man. In many other respects she was entirely suitable, being pious, prudish and virginal.

Hamilton could easily afford to give his pay packet to the tramp. He had been left quite a substantial amount of money and some valuable property, by the eccentric devout old lady, Mrs Latimer, who owned the Kilcalmonell estate. Her husband and two brothers had been killed in the 1914–1918 war. She had approved of his pacifist principles.

It was expected that he would soon go to Glasgow or Edinburgh to begin his studies. There he would meet some ladylike woman, perhaps a minister's widow, with influential family connections and two or three children. These would save him the trouble, not to mention the ordeal, of begetting some of his own, for if it was hard to imagine Miss Fiona in bed with a man it was just as hard to imagine Hamilton in bed with a woman.

Two

ONE SATURDAY, in June, when the sun was blazing on the loch and in all the hedges wild roses were in bloom, the forestry-workers' confabulation was interrupted by the appearance on the road of two decrepit creaky carts drawn by small shilpit horses, one of which seemed to be lame. On the first cart the reins were held by a grey-haired woman in a red cardigan. Huddled beside her was an old man wearing a hat. On the other cart were two children and a young woman. Her hair was short and raven-black. She was wearing thick dark trousers more suitable for a farm labourer and a black jumper that in itself was not remarkable but rather emphasised a bosom that was. What a waste, was a thought that occurred to more than one of the men, such fine breasts on a tinker girl who was no doubt unwashed and smelly, not to say skelly-eyed and with a mouthful of rotting teeth.

'Tinkers, by God,' cried Angus, the foreman. 'Where do they think they're going? We don't want their kind here. Human trash, and not so human at that, doing their business behind bushes, like animals.'

Other comments were not so bitter and contemptuous. But then, their only son had not been killed in the war.

'I believe there used to be a colony of them in Kilcalmonell.'

'That was a long time ago.'

'Their camps nowadays are up in Sutherland.'

'So they must have come a long way.'

'It shows. That first horse is lame.'

'The old fellow looks sound asleep.'

'Or dead.'

'Dead drunk,' cried Angus. 'They beg for money and then waste it on drink.'

There were chuckles. Angus himself was no Rechabite.

The carts had stopped. The young woman jumped down. She did it nimbly, though she was evidently very tired.

She patted the horse on its head and bent down to look at its leg. There was a fondness between them.

'Why have they stopped?'

'Maybe she wants to ask Mrs McTeague if she can use her toilet.'

'They don't need toilets. As Angus said they just piss behind bushes.'

There was laughter, some of it uneasy. They had daughters of their own.

'My God, she's coming over.'

'She must have heard it's pay day.'

'That's it,' cried Angus. 'She's coming to beg. Give her nothing, not a penny. Mind that, Hamilton.'

There were grins. If Hamilton decided to give the girl something, maybe his whole pay packet, he wouldn't ask for Angus's permission.

'Just look at her,' muttered Angus. 'You'd think she was proud of herself. Shameless young besom.'

She was walking with remarkable grace. She wasn't trying to provoke Angus. She did not know she was doing it.

All the same, thought Hamilton, Angus was right. Surely

she ought to be showing some shame, some humility anyway, considering how degrading a life she led, whether it was through her own fault or not. It must be stupidity.

Then she was close enough for him to see that, whatever it was, it wasn't stupidity. On the contrary, she looked too sensitive and intelligent for her own good. With increasing astonishment he saw that she was very good-looking. No, that was too tame a word; beautiful was more like it, ridiculous though it seemed. Her eyes were an unusual shade of brown and, in spite of her tiredness, were eager and alert. He was reminded of a deer. She had the same grace, the same air of wildness, as if she was poised to flee, into the forest and up onto the tops of the hills. As brown as a Native American, she was wearing a necklace of blue stones and pinned to her jumper between her breasts was a single white wild rose. As gestures of pride and self-respect they were insignificant but somehow very effective. Even Angus was finding it harder to wish her ill.

There was a whiff of dried sweat off her; it had been a hot day. She must know it, she must find it mortifying, but she still held up her head. She was having to pay for it, though. Hamilton saw her shiver once and for a few moments the light went out of her eyes.

'Wouldn't it have been better for her,' whispered old Dugald, 'if she'd been born glaikit-looking and humphy-backed? In the camps where she lives they'll be after her like dogs after a bitch in heat.' He sniggered.

And you'd be one of the pursuing dogs, thought Hamilton.

The boy on the cart shouted, 'I'm hungry, Effie.'

'I know, pet. We'll eat soon.'

'When did they last eat?' asked Hamilton.

She stared at him as if minded to ask what business it was of his. Instead she said, with a meekness that was obviously against her nature, 'Seven o'clock this morning.'

'That was more than five hours ago.'

'I do my best, Mister.' She was speaking in English. She had noticed his Gaelic was uncertain.

'I would like to speak to the man in charge,' she said.

The door of the hut opened and Hugh McTeague, the forester, appeared. 'That's me, lass. What can I do for you? If you need anything ask at the house. My wife will do what she can for you.'

He had two children of his own. His wife, Sheila, was sharp-tongued and good-hearted. She came from Glasgow, he from the isle of Eigg.

'We're not beggars,' said the girl. 'We can pay for what we need.'

There were some sceptical grins.

From her trouser pocket she took a small red tin that had once contained Oxo cubes. She opened it and revealed some small round objects that glowed in the sun.

'Pearls,' she said, 'Scottish pearls. We're not tinkers if that's what you've been thinking. We're pearl-fishers.'

'I've heard about the pearl fishing,' said McTeague. 'They're found in mussels, in rivers in Sutherland.'

'That's right.'

'How much are these worth?'

'I should get twenty pounds for them.'

There were gasps. It took a forestry worker ten weeks to earn as much.

'It took us four months to gather these. All of us.'

'Even the children?' asked Hamilton.

'I've been doing it since I was four.'

He was noticing how beautiful her hands were. Pure was the word that occurred to him. He thought of their immersion for many hours in the cold waters of Scottish rivers. If she kept doing it much longer those hands would lose their beauty and become swollen and contorted.

'We need the money for Grandfather's funeral,' she said.

'Is he as ill as that?' asked McTeague.

'We don't think he'll last another week.'

'In that case shouldn't he be in hospital?'

'He doesn't want to die in a hospital.'

'Why have you brought him here?'

'He was born in Kilcalmonell, eighty years ago. He wants to be buried here.'

There was some shaking of heads. The old fellow's soul might be welcome in heaven but his body wouldn't be in the kirkyard at Kilcalmonell, if Miss Fiona, the minister's sister, had anything to do with it.

'We need a place to camp,' she said. 'We'll pay.'

'I'm sorry I can't help you there, lass. At this time of year there's great danger of fire.'

'We heard there are sands on the loch. Couldn't we camp there?'

'No, you couldn't,' said Angus. 'People bring their children to play on those sands. They wouldn't want to be bothered with rubbish like you.'

He was ashamed that he had said it but he would say it again.

'That's not a very nice thing to say, Angus,' said McTeague.

'It was a very offensive thing to say,' said Hamilton, angrily. 'You should apologise, Angus.'

'To the likes of her? Never.'

If she was blushing it could not be seen for her tan, but

her voice trembled a little. 'We're not rubbish. Grandfather's a Gaelic poet. Men from universities have come to record him reciting his poems.'

'There's a field behind my house. You're welcome to camp there.'

It was Hamilton who had spoken.

She turned to him eagerly but asked with a trace of doubt in her voice. 'Whose land is it, Mister?'

'Mine. You would be safe there.'

'Wouldn't your wife object?'

'I'm not married.'

'You have no business encouraging them,' said Angus. 'That's what they do, send somebody like her on ahead, and then descend in dozens.'

'Only one man will come,' she said. 'For the funeral.'

'Is he your man?'

'What do you mean?'

'Are you his woman?'

'I'm nobody's woman. Did you mean it, Mister?'

'Yes, I meant it,' said Hamilton.

One of those beautiful hands was clenched against her breast.

'It's not far,' he said. 'Half a mile or so. Opposite the sands.'

'Are you sure about this, Gavin?' said McTeague. 'No disrespect to you, Miss, but this is not an ordinary house.'

'How many rooms is it again, Gavin?' someone asked. 'Ten or twelve?'

She looked in wonder at Hamilton, a forestry worker with so large a house.

'There are postcards with pictures of the Old Manse on them,' said McTeague.

'They can't camp in that field,' said Angus. 'People cross it on their way to the Chinese gardens. They won't want to walk past filthy tents.'

'What are the Chinese gardens?' asked the girl.

'Oh, it's just a name the local people give it,' said McTeague. 'It's the original water supply for the house. Half a dozen small reservoirs joined by hump-backed bridges. It is a beautiful place, to be sure.'

'We wouldn't have to go near them, would we?'

'No, you wouldn't,' said Hamilton. 'Tell me, what's your name?'

'Effie. Effie Williamson.'

'Mine's Gavin Hamilton.'

'We'll pay you, Mr Hamilton.'

'There's no need. I'll go on ahead and wait at the gate. You can't see the house from the road, because of the trees.'

He retrieved his bicycle from the tangle leaning against the hut. He gave the girl a nod and then wheeled his bicycle to the cart where the two children sat crouched together. He stopped and spoke to them briefly. Then he got on his bicycle and rode off.

'Has he really got a field?' asked the girl.

'Yes, indeed he has. It's where the schoolchildren hold their sports. You will be very comfortable there.'

'Does the house belong to him too?'

'Yes, but he has promised it to Glasgow Corporation as a holiday home for children from the slums.'

She turned to Angus. 'I'm sorry you don't like us, Mister. We don't mean any harm. After Grandfather's buried we'll go away and you'll never see us again.'

Angus turned his back on her.

'Excuse me,' she said, and walked proudly to the cart where her mother was watching anxiously.

'What was all that about, Effie?'

'It's all right. We've got a place to camp.'

'Where is it?'

'About half a mile along the road. Behind a big house.'

'Whose house? We don't want them setting their dogs on us.'

'It belongs to the man with the beard.'

'He was very interested in the children.'

'He was just concerned about them.'

'What's he charging for the use of his field?'

'Nothing. He said it wasn't necessary to pay.'

'I hope he's not one of those that wants something else from you.'

'He thinks too much of himself for that.'

'Is that so? If I get a chance I'll tell him to his face that the man that gets my Effie will be the luckiest man on God's earth.'

'Don't be silly, mother.'

Effie felt depressed. She had thought she could cope but was now afraid she couldn't. She had a headache. Her period had started. Things were getting too much for her. There was Grandfather dying, his funeral to arrange and pay for. He wanted to be buried in a certain place, in the forest, where his family had been buried eighty years ago. She didn't think it would be allowed. The old horse Maggie was lame. One of the cart wheels had developed a wobble. Morag wasn't well. The doctor in Tain had warned that she might slip into consumption if she didn't get proper food and rest. Daniel was coming, with a paper in his pocket, signed by Grandfather, giving him permission to marry Effie. With

Grandfather dead and no man in the family the authorities might take Morag and Eddie into care. They had threatened to do so. Effie's own hopes of escaping her present way of life were almost extinguished. Who would come and rescue her? No one in the whole world.

Trying to look cheerful, she went over to the children.

'Have we got a place to camp, Effie?' asked Morag.

'I think so, pet. The man with the beard that spoke to you, he said we could camp in a field behind his house.'

'Good. I liked him.' Morag was always too trusting.

'What did he say to you?'

'He just asked our names.'

'Will we get there soon, Effie?' said Eddie. 'I'm hungry.'

'We'll be there in ten minutes. We can't go very fast. Maggie's lame.'

They set off.

'Can we have tatties and sausages?' asked Eddie.

'I'm not sure about tatties. They take too long. But there's bread, new bread. You like that.'

In the baker's and the butcher's people had moved away discreetly.

The cart behind had stopped. Unable to wait any longer her mother was climbing down, with some difficulty. She crept behind some whin bushes at the side of the road. The thorns would catch in her skirt. She would probably wet herself.

Rubbish, the big man had called them. Effie sighed.

She was so relieved to see Hamilton waiting by an open gate that she almost burst into tears. She had been dreading that he had changed his mind. She should have felt grateful, and so she did, but she felt resentful too. She did not want to be beholden to him.

She looked down at him. 'Why are you doing this, Mr Hamilton? You'll get nothing from me.'

It was a stupid thing to say. What did she have that he would want?

Morag was smiling at him and he was smiling back. There was already an understanding between them. Effie felt shut out.

'If you really want to know,' he said, 'I'm doing it for the children.'

That was a reason she was willing to accept.

The second cart arrived.

Led by Hamilton, the two carts crunched up the gravel track, through the trees, and there suddenly was the house, built of sandstone, large and splendid.

'It's like a church, Effie,' whispered Morag.

They went round the side of the house, and there was the promised field, with lush grass and magnificent beech trees.

'I could play football here,' said Eddie.

There were stone outhouses, perhaps in the past they had been used as stables. They would be a shelter if there was heavy rain, but permission would have to be sought, and Effie would never seek it. Yonder was a rose garden, with a high fence round it to keep out deer.

Effie got down. Hamilton put up his hand to help her but she ignored it.

Morag and Eddie, though, were glad to accept his help.

Morag put her arms round his neck, as trusting as if he were her father.

Eddie ran off across the field, kicking an imaginary football.

'My God, Effie,' cried her mother, 'it's a bloody mansion.

Would you be so kind, Mister, as to give me a hand to get down? I'm as stiff as a tree.'

Effie went forward to help her mother but Hamilton was there before her.

It was almost as if he regarded himself as one of the family. He would have to be stopped.

Effie went and stood under one of the beech trees. Her legs were trembling. All of her was trembling. She was more intimidated by Hamilton's officious kindness than by the big man's abuse.

If she had been by herself she would have left immediately.

She could not have explained how he was doing it, perhaps he did not intend to do it, but Hamilton was taking from her in minutes what she had spent her life holding on to – not pride, for how could she be proud of the kind of life she led, but simply a resolution not to be ashamed or humiliated, for she had never done anything wrong nor harmed anyone.

So easily was he weakening that resolution.

Morag came and stood beside her. 'Is there anything wrong, Effie?'

'No, pet, there's nothing wrong.'

'This is a nice place, isn't it?'

'Very nice.'

'Can we stay here for a long time?'

'I don't think so.'

'I would like to stay here always. Wouldn't you, Effie?'

Effie took a deep breath and managed to smile. 'Yes, I think I would like to stay here always.'

Hamilton was coming to join them.

He spoke in English. He had already discovered that their English, even Eddie's, was better than his Gaelic.

'Do you hear the buzzards?'

They were mewing like cats as they soared higher and higher in the blue sky.

'They're often here. I love watching them. They're so joyful, so free.'

He was letting her know he was more interested in the birds than in her and her family.

'Excuse me,' she said. 'I'll have to see to the tents.'

'No.' He repeated it emphatically. 'No.'

She had been waiting for this. He had changed his mind and wanted them to leave.

It would be a terrible disappointment to the children, and to be truthful, to herself too.

Then, to her utter astonishment, he said, 'I want you to sleep in the house, all of you.'

Morag clapped her hands in delight. 'Oh, I would like that. Wouldn't you, Effie?'

Effie was staring at Hamilton. 'What are you trying to do? Are you trying to take away what little pride we have left?'

'What pride, for God's sake?' cried her mother. 'One thing our kind can't afford is pride.'

She saw that Effie had gone into one of her ominous silences. God knew what went on in her mind then.

'She's my daughter but I can't say I understand her.'

He thought he could. After a week or so living in a house and sleeping in a proper bed, Effie would know how purgatorial it must be having to go back, perhaps for the rest of her life, to crawling on hands and knees into a small dark smelly tent, like an animal into its burrow.

Mrs Williamson took him aside. 'I've got a favour to ask you, Mister, two favours. Do you have any whisky in the house?'

'No.'

'But could you get some? Grandfather needs it to help him sleep.'

It was probably the truth.

'I could get some if it was really necessary.'

'It's necessary all right. The second thing's a wee bit delicate, you not being a married man. Effie's having her period and we've run out of clean clouts. If there's a woman where you're going would you ask her if we could have one or two sanitary towels? For God's sake, say nothing about this to Effie.'

Poor Effie, he thought.

'While you're away I'll talk to Effie.'

'Tell her I want you to use the house as if you were my guests.'

She laughed. 'Some guests.'

'There are two bathrooms, one upstairs. Use the kitchen. There's some food in the larder. You're welcome to it.'

'Thanks, Mister. There's Morag coughing again. You'll have noticed she's not very well. We don't expect her to be long after Grandfather.'

He hurried away. There were tears in his eyes. He already loved that little girl.

Mrs Williamson shook her head as she watched him go. He was a good man but like all good people he was simple, easy to take in.

She had her own plans ready. All right, they were selfish, but who could blame her? Daniel was coming, to claim his bride, as he thought. He wasn't going to be disappointed, except that his bride wasn't going to be Effie, who had rejected him a dozen times and would do it again. He would have to be content with her, Nellie Williamson, as he ought to be, for they had slept together often enough. In fact,

Morag was his; they had the same pale blue eyes and fair hair. They would get married properly, in a church, and she'd be wearing white, with a bouquet of lilies. They would live in his nice little cottage outside Tain, and she'd help him run his scrap iron business.

If Morag and Eddie had to be taken into care, what of it? They'd be looked after well enough there.

As for Effie, if she was lucky she might land a job, as a hospital cleaner, say, or she might he bullied into marrying some drunken lout who'd give her half a dozen kids and many beatings. Yes, that could be poor Effie's fate. A great pity but it couldn't be helped.

Three

HE COULD have gone on his bicycle and still more quickly in his car, but he preferred to walk. He wanted time to think about his visitors, whose coming, he was convinced, was not accidental. They had been sent to him, surely for a purpose.

He felt exhilarated. All doubts, inhibitions and feelings of unworthiness were gone. Degrading ppl.

He stopped to look at the wild roses in the hedge, remembering the one on Effie's breast, by now wilting and falling to pieces. He would replace it with the most beautiful rose in his garden. His hands trembled at the thought.

It was much too simple to say that he had fallen in love with her.

It was the McTeague children who opened the door.

'It's Uncle Gavin,' they shouted to their mother in the kitchen.

'Did you bring the tinker children?' asked seven-year-old Ian.

'Don't be silly,' said his sister. 'Just because they're camping in his field doesn't mean they belong to him.'

Their mother appeared, looking very fresh and clean. She was as great a contrast to Effie as her happy and healthy children were to shy sickly Morag and Eddie with his false confidence. Tall and fair, she was wearing an immaculate white blouse and a tweed skirt protected by an apron with Scottish scenes depicted on it. He thought of Effie's workman's trousers and boots, and the smell of dried sweat.

'Sit down, Gavin,' she said, 'and tell me about your visitors. I'm sure you're in no hurry to get back to them, so why not join us at lunch? The old man hasn't died, has he?'

'No.'

'You two go and tell your father lunch will be ready in ten minutes.'

The children went, grumbling. They wanted to hear about the tinker children.

'You will, later. Maybe if Gavin doesn't mind we'll visit them tomorrow afternoon.

'Now, Gavin, tell me about this tinker girl.'

'She's not a tinker, she's a pearl-fisher.'

'So Hugh told me. But we'll all think of her as the tinker girl all the same. They lead the same kind of lives, don't they? Hugh says she's quite handsome, underneath the dirt.'

'She's not got a nice bathroom with hot water.'

Sheila laughed at his indignation.

'What's her name?'

'Effie. Effie Williamson.'

'Hugh said he liked the way she stood up to Angus.'

'Angus was unforgivably rude. And she would stand up to anyone. She's very brave.'

'Brave? Well, I suppose it would take a lot of nerve to travel from Sutherland on a cart with two children, sleeping in a tent in all kinds of lonely places. Have they got their tents up in your field?'

'No, they won't need them. I've invited them to sleep in the house.'

'Good heavens, Gavin, was that wise? I was about to ask if you'd remembered to lock your doors.'

'They're not thieves.'

'Maybe not, but they do get that reputation, don't they? And you've got such valuable pieces of furniture. I hate to think of them being damaged.'

God forgive her, she thought of the tinker children climbing up onto that magnificent chiffonier, like little animals let loose.

'Effie wouldn't allow it. Anyway, they're not mischievous children.'

'Don't be surprised if you get a visit from the police.'

'What have the police got to do with it?'

'Isn't it against the law nowadays for children of that age not to be sent to school? I'm surprised they haven't been taken into care already. I don't suppose the girl can read and write. There could be complaints.'

One was likely to come from Miss Fiona, the minister's sister. She wouldn't be acting in the children's interests.

'Gavin, I'm going to speak frankly. I realise you can't just order them to leave, but don't interfere. Leave them alone. You know better than anyone else how easy it is to hurt people when your intention is to help them. Another thing. You're a bit of a simpleton where women, and children too, are concerned. That girl, Effie, will probably try to take advantage of you.'

'What do you mean?'

'You know fine what I mean. You're not as simple as that.'

'She's not like that.'

'How do you know what she's like?'

He got to his feet. He wanted to get back to present that rose to Effie.

'Have you any whisky you could let me have?'

'Whisky?'

'It seems the old man needs it to help him sleep.'

I suppose it's true, she thought, as she went into the kitchen.

She came back with a half bottle of whisky three-quarters full.

'It's all we've got. With Hugh's compliments.'

'Thanks, Sheila, and thank Hugh.' He lowered his voice. 'There's another thing. Mrs Williamson said that Effie's having her period and they've got no sanitary towels left. They'd be grateful if you could let them have one or two till Monday.'

She couldn't help laughing. 'Hugh and I have been married twelve years but I can't imagine him going on such an errand for me. Good for you, Gavin.'

She went off and came back with an unopened packet. 'With *my* compliments. Put it in your pocket. Poor girl.'

'Yes, she deserves a better life. She needs someone to rescue her before it's too late.'

'I hope you're not thinking of being that someone.'

'Why not? They were sent to me.'

Did he really believe that? She couldn't be sure.

Luckily she didn't have to comment for just then her husband and children came into the house.

She sent the children to wash their hands at once.

McTeague was jovial. 'Hello, Gavin. How are you getting on with your visitors?'

'They're no trouble. I've just come to borrow some whisky, Hugh. It's for the old man. He needs it to help him sleep. I'd better be getting back.'

Sheila saw him to the door. 'Would you mind, Gavin, if I brought the children to visit you tomorrow afternoon? I could bring some clothes that they've grown out of.'

'You'd have to be tactful, Sheila. Effie's very proud.'

What in heaven's name has she to be proud about? thought Sheila. 'I promise to be very tactful,' she said.

She hurried back to the living room. 'Would you believe it, he's invited them to sleep in the house.'

Her husband often surprised her with his reactions.

'Well, why not? He's plenty of beds.'

'But they're bound to be filthy.'

'Well, he's got two bathrooms.'

'But it's ridiculous. He's gone too far this time. Do you know what he said? He said they'd been sent to him. I think he meant it.'

'Did he say who sent them?'

'He must have meant God, of course.'

'Well, considering that everything that's done is done by God he must be right then.'

'You're not taking this seriously. What if they decide to stay and he can't get rid of them?'

'I suppose he'd just have to wait till God sent them away again.'

'It's not a joke, Hugh. They could be there for weeks.'

'Months,' said McTeague, cheerfully. 'Isn't the house going to be used as a holiday home for poor children? Well, those children are very poor and they need a holiday. They will do Gavin a lot of good; especially the young woman. He's probably thinking that this is the best opportunity he's ever had to show what a good Christian he is. She won't let herself be used in that way.'

'She seems a remarkable young woman.'

'She is. She's got character. You should've seen her standing up to Angus.'

Four

THE FORESTER had not been joking when he had said that the Old Manse was not an ordinary house.

Built in Victorian times, when Highland ministers had large families, some as many as a dozen, and when the Church of Scotland had been important and influential, the best materials had been used, expense no object. There were stained glass windows depicting scenes from the life of Christ and a grand mahogany staircase that would not have been out of place in Kilcalmonell House itself.

The lighting back then had been by oil lamps. A careless maidservant had one day caused a fire which had destroyed part of the roof and the upper part of the house. To repair it would have cost too much. A new manse, more manageable and less ambitious was built closer to the church. In any case the congregation by that time was greatly decreased. The population of Kilcalmonell itself had shrunk from over five hundred to less than a hundred. The Old Manse was abandoned. Trees soon shrouded it. Its very existence was forgotten.

One day, out walking, Gavin Hamilton had caught a glimpse of it among the trees. On a smaller scale he had felt the same thrill as those explorers who had come across the temples in the jungle in Cambodia. He had ventured in and like them had been greatly impressed. It had struck him that restoring it would be a work blessed by God.

He had gone to Mrs Latimer, who was then owner of the estate. She liked the idea of rebuilding at a time when there was so much destruction in the world. She was willing to pay for the materials, but where were they going to find the workmen, in a time of war? This didn't turn out to be the problem they had anticipated.

Among the pacifists sent to work in the forest there were skilled craftsmen, mostly hailing from Glasgow, who were keen on the idea of restoring the house and offering it to their native city as a holiday home for children from the slums. They took no wages and worked hard during their spare time. News spread. There was an article in a Glasgow paper. People sent donations.

It was agreed that the manse would be restored as a family home, and not as a charitable institution. There would be no indoctrination of the children. No uniforms would be worn, though wellingtons and raincoats might have to be issued. When an artist among them volunteered to put paintings on the ceilings, it was considered a good idea, but only if the paintings had nothing to do with religion. He suggested scenes from *Treasure Island* and *Kidnapped*. As a joke he painted Long John Silver to look like Gavin Hamilton.

About a quarter of a mile from the house a military lookout post had been constructed. Water and power had to be supplied to it, whatever the expense and effort, and the pipes and wires had passed close to the Old Manse. Soon after the end of the war it had been easy to persuade the authorities to divert the water and electricity into the house.

It was an excellent spot for its purpose. There was the big field where football and other games could be played. There were the sands. There was Towellan to visit. There were hills to wander over.

Off-duty soldiers had been glad to lend a hand.

There had been a proposal to call it Latimer House, in honour of Mrs Latimer but she had wanted it to keep its old name.

Though it was ultimately to be handed over to Glasgow Corporation, Mrs Latimer insisted that it should first be made the property of Gavin Hamilton. It was now worth a good deal of money, and she had been afraid that her only living heir, a nephew who lived in England, might want it to remain the property of the estate.

Five

MRS WILLIAMSON was wishing that the house was a lot smaller and less grand. She would not have been so scared to go into it. Not even its owner could give the likes of her permission. Hamilton hadn't warned her that he had a dog, a big fierce one, but owners of houses like this one always had such dogs to chase off riff-raff like her. Then there were the police who had often turned up and ordered her and her family out of broken-down sheds hardly fit for sheep.

There were not many places where they were welcome.

But she had to get Grandfather off the cart and put him somewhere where he could lie down. He must be stiff and sore from sitting on the cart for hours. Besides, he had wet himself.

'For God's sake, Effie,' she muttered, 'come and help me.'

But there was Effie pushing Eddie on a swing they had found hanging from one of the beech trees. He was screaming with glee, for, to tell the truth, he wasn't quite right in the head. From a distance Effie looked as if she was enjoying herself, big sister playing with little brother, but Mrs Williamson had never known her so unhappy, so despairing, so close to weeping. Meeting Hamilton had reminded her of what she would miss all her life.

'Effie,' yelled her mother, 'come and help me with Grandfather.'

Effie pretended not to have heard.

She would never forgive Grandfather for trying to make her marry Daniel. She had said she would kill herself first. Not an empty threat, for her grandmother, also called Effie, had crawled out of the tent one dark wet November night and never come back. Three days later she had been found drowned in the river. She had been nineteen.

Morag was telling Effie that their mother wanted her.

Though only ten, Morag was the peacemaker. She had the sweetest nature of any child Mrs Williamson had ever known. They hadn't needed old Bella the spaewife to tell them that Morag would never scart a grey head, meaning that she would die young. She would look sad and peaceful in her white coffin. Effie's heart would break.

Hand in hand they came across to their mother.

'If you're not going to put up a tent, Effie, we'll have to get Grandfather into the house. He needs to lie down and he needs to be changed. He's pissed himself.'

'Well, take him in.'

'I'm scared, Effie. I'm not brave like you. There could be a dog, and the police could come. Don't forget I've a lot more experience than you of being attacked by dogs and ordered away by police.'

'Didn't Hamilton give you permission?'

'I know but I'm still scared. It's so big.'

'It's just a house. Even if it was ten times as big it would still be just a house. Houses are for people. We're people, aren't we? We're not animals.'

But Mrs Williamson knew that when she went into the

house she would look more like a skulking animal than a person with permission.

'I'll go in with you, Effie,' said Morag, 'but I think you should take off your boots. We don't want to cause any damage.'

Laughing, Effie bent and embraced her sister.

'They're tackety boots, Effie.'

'So they are. All right, I'll take them off. I'll pretend I'm going into a heathen temple.'

'What do you mean?'

'Never mind, pet. It was just a joke.'

Morag was always slow to see a joke. When she did see it she seldom found it funny.

Effie knelt and took off her boots. Her feet were shapely and strong but they might have been cleaner. She seldom wore socks.

Barefooted she went boldly in, determined not to feel too impressed. It was just a house.

Morag tiptoed. She stretched up her arms. 'I couldn't do this in a tent,' she said.

'No, pet, you couldn't.'

They found themselves in the hall at the front of the house. On the parquet floor were coloured reflections from a stained glass window that depicted Christ and a lamb in a field of flowers. On the ceiling Long John Silver and his band of villains brandished cutlasses and muskets.

Morag noticed. 'Is that because this is Mr Hamilton's house?'

'I think it was meant as a joke.'

There was an imposing staircase leading up to the bedrooms. Shall I go up there tonight, Effie thought, or shall I sleep outside in a tent?

She was in danger of feeling sorry for herself.

They opened a door. It was a bedroom, probably Hamilton's. The bed was unmade, his pyjamas were lying on it.

For a few silly, guilty, shameful moments Effie shut her eyes and pretended that she and Hamilton were married and had shared that bed last night.

She opened her eyes again and faced reality. Reality was her headache, her tiredness, her disgust with herself, and her dirty feet.

'Are you all right, Effie?'

'Yes, pet, I'm fine.'

'Do you think there's a lavatory?'

'I'm sure there is.'

'Would it be all right if I used it?'

'Of course.'

'I won't make a mess.'

'You never do.'

They opened another door, and there was the bathroom.

It was very clean and had blue tiles but it was not fancy. Hamilton's toiletries were on a shelf.

Morag sat down daintily. She did everything daintily.

Her last lavatory had been a whin bush with bees buzzing among the yellow flowers. It had not been so comfortable, she thought, but it had been more interesting.

'I would like to have a bath, Effie.'

'So would I. Well, maybe a shower. A bath takes too long.'

The next room they same upon was the sitting room. It was large, with armchairs and sofas. There was a sideboard with a vase of roses on it. There was a glass-fronted book-case full of books.

'We've got no books, Effie.'

'No.'

'Is that because we can't read?'

'I can read.'

'I've never seen you reading a book, Effie.'

Effie felt dismayed and ashamed.

'Never mind, Effie, maybe Mr Hamilton will teach you.'

Six

THERE FOLLOWED a busy half-hour.

Effie and Morag had their shower, using Hamilton's soft white towels rather than their own hard dingy ones: they would take his to the laundry on Monday. Eddie brought in the Primus and the battered tin plates and cooking utensils. They were to use their own things and not Hamilton's. Grandfather, still with his hat on, was seated in an armchair in a corner of the kitchen, waiting for the whisky. Effie, wearing Hamilton's apron over her red dress, was the cook. Morag assisted her.

They were seated at the table when Hamilton came in. He had a yellow rose in his hand.

'This is for you, Effie, to replace the one you had this morning.'

A variety of expressions crossed her face. She looked puzzled, pleased, amused and embarrassed.

He could not keep his eyes off her. Gone was the ragamuffin in the black jumper and thick trousers. In her place was a handsome elegant young lady in a red dress and a yellow cardigan. There was a neat darn in the right elbow. He had never seen anything more moving.

She picked up the rose and smelled it. 'What a lovely scent. Smell it, Morag.'

Morag smelled it. 'Me and Effie took a shower in your bathroom, Mr Hamilton. We didn't make a mess.'

'I'm sure you didn't.'

'We used your towels. Effie didn't want to but I said you wouldn't mind.'

'Of course I don't mind.' He handed the bottle of whisky to Mrs Williamson.

'Thanks, Mister. I knew you wouldn't forget.'

She was about to pour whisky into two tin mugs.

Hamilton laughed. 'You can't drink whisky out of those.' He got two whisky glasses out of a cupboard.

'Grandfather once drank it out of a silver tassie, in Carbisdale Castle. Didn't you, Grandfather?'

The old man raised his glass to Hamilton. It was a strangely dignified gesture. Hamilton could believe the man was a poet.

'We kept a sausage for you, Mr Hamilton,' said Eddie. 'If you don't want it can I have it?'

'Sorry, Eddie. I'm hungry.'

He sat down at the table, beside Morag.

Effie served him the sausage and bread soaked in dripping. She used a china plate she got down from a shelf.

'Are you sure you want this?' she asked.

'Of course I want it.'

Mrs Williamson was winking at him. She was asking if he had remembered the other thing.

He nodded. He was trying to look as if he was enjoying the sausage and bread. 'Well, what would you like to do this afternoon? I'm going shopping. Who would like to come with me?'

'Me,' said Eddie, 'but I've got no money.'

'I'll lend you some. What about you, Effie? Have you any shopping to do?'

'Is there a bus?'

'I'm afraid there's just one bus a day. It leaves the head

of the loch in the morning and returns from Towellan in
the late afternoon. It carries sheep as well as people. We'll
have to go in the car.'

'Good,' said Eddie.

'I thought we might go to the matinee at the cinema.'

'I would like that,' said Morag.

'Then that's what we'll do. I'll go and have a shower and
change my clothes. I'll be ready in twenty minutes.'

Effie followed him out. She spoke quietly so that the
others wouldn't hear.

'I have to talk to you, Mr Hamilton.'

'If I call you Effie why don't you call me Gavin?'

'I can't. I know you're trying to be kind, but you shouldn't,
you mustn't.'

'Why not?'

'The children are already too fond of you.'

'What's wrong with that, for heaven's sake?'

'Because we're different.'

'I'm surprised at you, Effie. Just because you're poor and
your people have chosen to travel about and live in tents
doesn't mean you're inferior.'

'I didn't say inferior, I said different.'

'But, Effie, you've given me the impression that you would
like to change your way of life.'

'My way of life is none of your business, Mr Gavin
Hamilton.'

She rushed away then, with a small cry of anguish.

He stood listening. His heart was beating fast. He had
ventured too dangerously.

She seemed to have gone outside.

He went into the kitchen. Here was his chance to give
Mrs Williamson the pads.

Morag and Eddie were washing and drying the tin dishes. Grandfather and Mrs Williamson were happily drowsy.

'With Mrs McTeague's compliments,' he said, putting the packet on the table.

'Who's she?'

'A friend. Where's Effie?'

He looked out of the window. There was Effie, with her head close to that of the old grey horse.

He must heed her warning. There could be no place in his future for her.

Seven

IN THE car Eddie sat up front beside Hamilton, pretending he was driving. Morag was in the back with Effie. Both were very quiet, except for Morag's occasional cough.

It looked as if he and Effie had decided to find a way of behaving towards each other that wouldn't cause embarrassment. They would be friendly but not close. She would live in the house, for the children's sake. She would call him Gavin. Somehow she felt that calling him Mr Hamilton would look as if she was too deliberately trying to keep a safe distance between them.

For his part, he was going to be very careful not to hurt her feelings but at the same time not to give her foolish hopes. There must be no more inane gestures like giving her the rose. He had almost found himself offering to pin it on her breast.

Suddenly she spoke, in a carefully controlled tone of voice. This was how she was going to speak to him from now on.

'Do you know a place called the Big Stone?'

He tried to copy her emotionless tone. It was harder for him because he liked and admired her, and would have liked to show it, whereas to her he was simply a self-important person trying to show how good he was.

'Yes, it's in the forest, not far from Mr McTeague's house. As a matter of fact we'll pass it soon. We won't be able to see it, though, because of trees. It's said people were buried there. There are signs of graves. Why?'

'That's where Grandfather wants to be buried. The graves are those of his family – his father and mother, and his brother. Eighty years ago. They all died in the same week.'

'God! Was it an accident?'

'They just got ill and died. It had been a bad winter for them. They hadn't enough food. It could have been pneumonia. Grandfather was only four and he doesn't remember it very well.'

'Did nobody help?'

'I think they were afraid it was something smittle and they kept away.'

'How awful it must have been for the little boy.'

'He's made poems about it.'

'And you've brought him all this way to give him his wish? You're a heroine, Effie.'

'Do you think they'll allow him to be buried there?'

'I don't know. It's forestry land now. It belonged to the estate then. I don't think Hugh McTeague would object but his superiors might. Also the local health authorities might have something to say.'

'If it wasn't allowed, could he be buried in the kirkyard at Kilcalmonell? He said that would do as well.'

The honest answer was no. Robert McDonald, the minister, wouldn't mind but his sister Fiona certainly would, and most of the members would agree with her.

He slowed down the car. 'If you were visiting the Big Stone, this is where you'd have to climb the fence. It's a boggy area. There are lots of marigolds.'

He drove on. 'The man to ask would be Mr Rutherford. His family have been undertakers in Towellan for generations.'

They were now on the outskirts of the town.

'Would you please let us off here?' said Effie.

'Wouldn't it be better outside the hotel? That's more central.'

'No. Here would do.'

He realised that she didn't want any of his friends to see him with the tinkers. For his sake. She would keep the unspoken agreement more honourably than he.

He got out to help the children down. He was careful not to offer his hand to Effie.

He gave Eddie and Morag a shilling each.

'There's no need,' said Effie. 'We'll have money when I sell some of the pearls.'

'Shall we meet outside the cinema at a quarter to three?' he asked.

She hesitated. 'I'm not sure.'

'Well, I'll be there.'

He drove on and got out at the hotel.

He looked back eagerly. There they were, the three of them, strangers in this place, outcasts indeed.

He wished he was with them, that he had a right to be with them. But of course if that right was on offer he could not accept it.

One of his workmates was approaching, with his wife.

Archie McLeish was a good-natured man who agreed with everybody; his wife Meg made up for it by being deliberately cantankerous.

'Hello, Gavin,' said Archie, with his usual complaisant grin. 'How are you getting on with your tinks?'

'They're no trouble.'

'They shouldn't be allowed to live like that in this day and age,' said Meg. 'Especially if they have children with them.'

'They've been living like that for centuries,' said Archie. 'It's in their blood. I was telling Meg the young woman was quite good-looking.'

'They get gey coarse as they get older,' said Meg. 'No wonder. How long do you think you'll have them?'

'I don't know.'

'If it wasn't for the children I'd say get rid of them at once.'

She had three children of her own.

They moved on and Hamilton looked again for Effie and the children. They weren't to be seen. Perhaps they were in the jeweller's, selling the pearls.

Again he wished he was with them. But Effie would not be easily swindled and in any case Mr Lojko would offer a fair price.

Hamilton went off to have a talk with Mr Rutherford, the undertaker.

Eight

MR RUTHERFORD was a tall, thin, bald man with a very soft voice.

He listened attentively.

'Of course, Mr Hamilton, I know about those graves at the Big Stone.'

He got up and took down from a shelf one of a number of ledgers.

'What year did you say?'

'1870 or 1871.'

Mr Rutherford turned the stiff yellowish pages. 'Yes, here it is. The entry is by my grandfather, now of course deceased. Most meticulous. No typewriters in those days. "1870. 3rd December. Burial, at the Big Stone, in the grounds of the Kilcalmonell estate, of one Edward Williamson, an itinerant mendicant. His spouse, Agnes Williamson, and their son, aged six. Cause of death? Question mark. No religious service. Total cost 20 guineas. Paid by public subscription."'

'Were they trying to make amends?' said Hamilton, bitterly.

'So, Mr Hamilton, the one member of the family who survived and who was only four years of age at the time, has been brought to Kilcalmonell to be buried beside them. He is not, however, deceased, but is not expected to live much longer. That is the situation?'

'Yes, do you think it will be allowed?'

'I would have to make enquiries . . . You may be assured, I am very sympathetic. You say you are here on behalf of the granddaughter.'

'Yes.'

'She is herself an itinerant?'

'Yes.'

'I believe she passed through the town this morning, on a cart.'

'Yes.'

'She cannot be particularly well-off.'

'No.'

'An interment of this sort could be costly. Lawyers might have to be employed.'

'The bill would be paid.'

'May I ask, Mr Hamilton, what is your personal interest in the matter? You are not, I assume, related to these people?'

'No, I'm not. They need help. That's my interest.'

'Most commendable. We should all follow your example.'

'Could you let me know as soon as possible the result of your enquiries?'

'There is no telephone at the Old Manse?'

'Not yet. Mr McTeague the forester would take a message. He will probably be involved in any case.'

'Perhaps I could meet Miss Williamson?'

'Yes, of course.'

Nine

THERE WAS no need to hurry, he had plenty of time, but he hurried all the same. He felt pleased with himself, and was looking forward, not to receiving Effie's thanks, but to seeing some of the worry leave those beautiful, brave, brown eyes. She might at first protest that she had no right to expect him to take up a burden that really was no business of his, but she was bound to feel relieved and grateful afterwards.

People were already going into the cinema, many of them children. They looked so happy and carefree, so confident and healthy, laughing and chattering among themselves, that he thought sadly of Morag and Eddie, especially of Morag with her mouse-like diffidence and pale eager face.

It seemed to be a popular film. The cinema would be packed. Just in case, he went in and bought two adult and two children's tickets. Then he went outside again to wait.

He would sit between Eddie and Morag, so that he would not be too close to Effie, although he would have liked to sit beside her.

His heart took a sudden leap. What lay ahead for Effie?

It seemed inconceivable that in a week's time, perhaps sooner, she would slip out of Kilcalmonell as suddenly as she had arrived and set out on an arduous and perilous journey of two hundred miles to some bleak campsite, beside one of the rivers where she fished for pearls. She would be back to her old way of life. It would be as if she and Hamilton had never met. It was inconceivable and yet it would happen. She would, as Meg McLeish had said, grow coarse. Worse than that, she would give up hope of escape. For the children's sake she would marry one of her own clan who might be kind to her but would never appreciate her as she deserved. She would bear children.

Would he, in Glasgow or Edinburgh, an ordained minister, ready to fulfil his ambitions, remember her?

It was now past the meeting time. He looked in each direction. Towellan was going about its usual Saturday afternoon business. People were meeting friends and chatting. Some were going into shops, others were coming out. There were lots of screaming seagulls. But there was no sign of Effie and the children. Perhaps she was in a shop and had forgotten. She had no watch.

Nearly an hour later, with the cinema entrance deserted, he gave up.

So keen was his disappointment he felt resentful and, God forgive him, vindictive. Who did she think she was? He had known that she was proud, though God knew what she had to be proud about, but he had not known she was also arrogant. But why was he surprised? Uneducated and ignorant, how could she be expected to behave like a civilised person?

Had she decided, without bothering to consult him, that he would not want to be seen with her and the children in a public place like the cinema? Or was it that she didn't want to be seen with him?

His friends would say, laughing, 'Look, there's Gavin doing his Christian duty, being nice to the tinks.'

She would never let herself be used in that way.

These were his thoughts as he stood outside the cinema, surveying the streets full of people but empty for him.

Let her go. Let her, if she could, find another place to camp. He would miss the children and, he felt sure, they would miss him, but it couldn't be helped.

He went into the chemist's to buy medicine that would alleviate Morag's cough and then into a newsagent's for comics for Eddie.

The children were not to blame for their sister's arrogance.

In the licensed grocer's he arranged to have two bottles of whisky included in his weekly order that Willie would leave at the Old Manse gate.

The old man too was not to blame.

They would go back on Willie's bus. A taxi would be too dear. Someone would have told them that the bus left from outside the hotel at four o'clock.

He watched from a safe distance.

The bus arrived at ten to four. There they were, hurrying to it. Willie came off to help them aboard. Hamilton was pleased. Willie would look after them.

Why had his own reaction been so extreme and angry? No one in the world was less arrogant than Effie.

He would watch the bus leave then hurry back home to see them.

Ten

TOWELLAN ATTRACTED many holidaymakers, so its inhabitants were accustomed to seeing strangers in their streets and shops. Even so, Effie and the children were given more than their share of curious stares. It was now general knowledge that tinks had passed through the town that morning. Among them had been a young woman and two children. And now, here they were, back in the town, trying to act as if they were no different from other visitors.

After an hour or so of wandering about, and going in and out of shops, Effie and the children were glad to find refuge and rest in a small tearoom up a side street. That was where they were when they should have been outside the cinema meeting Hamilton.

Eddie was in a huff. He had been looking forward to the cinema and was cross with Effie. Morag was concerned that Mr Hamilton would be waiting for nothing.

They spoke in Gaelic, to the amusement of the waitress and other customers.

'You'd have fallen asleep,' said Effie. 'Look, you can hardly keep your eyes open.'

She was finding it difficult to justify her robbing them of a rare pleasure.

It was easy and truthful enough to say that they were too tired.

The real reasons were more complex. Yes, she had not wanted to be seen in such a public place with Hamilton, both for his sake, for his friends would laugh at him, and for her own, because she did not want to be more obliged to him than she already was.

But that was not the main reason.

The humiliating truth was that she was afraid of falling in love with him. If she did, if she let it happen, she would for the rest of her life not be able to forget him and what he could have represented for her.

In her ten-year-old way Morag was already in love with him. Therefore she vaguely sympathised with her big sister, but was also a little jealous. She could not resist teasing Effie.

'Mr Hamilton isn't married, is he, Effie?'

'You know he isn't. We wouldn't be in his house if he was.'

'Why isn't he? He's very good-looking and he's got a big house.'

'And a car,' added Eddie, who kept yawning.

'Perhaps he hasn't met anyone he wanted to marry.'

'But he will one day, won't he?'

'I expect so.'

'What kind of woman will she be?'

'Goodness, how should I know?'

'She'll be very good-looking.'

'He may think good looks aren't important.'

'She'll wear hats and go to church.'

Effie had to smile. 'I'm sure she will.'

'She'll read books.'

'Probably.'

'She'll wear nice clothes.'

'So she will.'

'She'll smell nice.'

'She'll be able to afford expensive perfumes.'

'I think she'll be lucky. Do you think she'll be lucky, Effie?'

'Very lucky.'

'If I was your age, Effie, I'd want to marry him myself. Would you like to marry him?'

'Not me. Do you know why?'

'No. Why?'

'I don't like men with beards.'

'But his is such a nice beard.'

'What are you two talking about?' asked Eddie. He was almost asleep.

'Effie, are you going to marry Daniel?'

'I don't think so.'

'That's why he's coming, isn't it?'

'He's coming to attend grandfather's funeral. Would you like me to marry him?'

'No. He's too old.'

'He gives me money,' muttered Eddie.

'When you're married, Effie, will you have children of your own?'

'I suppose so. That's why people get married.'

'How many will you have?'

'Dozens.'

'I'm being serious, Effie.'

'Well, say three.'

'You wouldn't want us then, me and Eddie, would you?'

'Don't be silly. Of course I would. I love you both. You're my sister and brother.'

'Half-sister and half-brother. Maybe the person you marry, Effie, won't want us.'

Such a person was Daniel. He would put the children into care.

Effie looked at the clock on the wall.

'We'd better go or we'll miss the bus.'

'We don't need the bus,' said Eddie. 'We can go in Mr Hamilton's car.'

'We can't,' said Morag. 'Effie's not friends with Mr Hamilton.'

'Why is she not friends with him?'

'I don't know. You'd better ask her.'

But Effie just smiled and shook her head.

At the hotel they were in good time for the bus.

Before she got on board Effie furtively glanced about, looking for Hamilton. Of course he wasn't there. She had some cheek thinking he might be.

He was in the kitchen, putting away the groceries, when there was a knock on the door; not the main door but the one the servants must have used. There were stairs leading up to the attics where they had slept. It was to ensure that they did not have to appear in the main part of the house. Those men of God, those Church of Scotland ministers with their large families, had been autocratic as well as lustful.

'Come in,' he called.

It was Effie. She had been crying.

He had a great desire to take her in his arms.

'Come in, Effie. Sit down. Is there anything the matter?'

What a fatuous question, he thought. There were so many things the matter with poor Effie.

'Did you get a good price for the pearls? Would you like some tea?'

'No thanks.'

She was wearing her red dress. The yellow flower he had given her was pinned to her breast.

'Where's everybody?'

'They're all asleep. I wanted to talk to you.'

He waited, smiling.

'We want to leave.'

He was astonished and dismayed. 'I thought you were happy here.'

'That's why.'

'I don't understand, Effie.'

She spoke with quiet passion. 'We've been attacked by dogs, and bitten. We've had our tents set on fire. We've had stones thrown at us, and we've been called trash, but it's you, Gavin Hamilton, who's done us the most harm.'

'In what way, Effie?'

'You've made it impossible for us, for me anyway, to go back to our old ways.'

He had been so pleased with himself, so democratic and Christian, that he hadn't considered the effect his generosity would have on them.

'I think I would like tea after all . . . There's something else I want to say. Those men at the hut, they were all thinking they could have me if they wanted. For half a crown.'

'Not all of them, Effie.'

'I don't care whether you believe me or not, it's not important, but no man has ever had me.'

'I do believe you, Effie.'

And so he did. She might live in squalor, she might be miserably poor, but she had kept her self-respect.

He had thought her remarkable before. Now he was learning just how remarkable she was.

'But I thought, Effie, you didn't want to go back to your old ways.'

'I don't, but what else can I do?'

'I don't want you to leave, Effie.'

He was in danger of giving promises he would never be able to keep.

'If we stay for a little while, we'll keep out of your way.'

The tea was ready. He poured it out.

'I had a talk with Mr Rutherford, the undertaker, about burial at the Big Stone.'

'What did he say? Does he think it will be allowed?'

'He's going to make enquiries.'

'Did he say how much it would cost?'

'No.'

'I could borrow from Daniel.'

'Who *is* this Daniel, Effie?'

'His name's Daniel Stewart. He's known me all my life. He used to be a pearl-fisher but he's got a business now. He's quite well off for a traveller. He wants to marry me.'

'How old is he?'

'About fifty.'

'You can't marry a man as old as that. Do you love him?'

'No, I don't. When Grandfather dies there will be no man in the family. I've been told the children might be taken from me and put in a home. I would do anything to prevent that. Daniel's promised that if we were married he'd let the children live with us.'

'Would he keep his promise?'

'I don't think so.'

'So you could find yourself married to a man thirty years older than you, whom you don't love, and yet still have the children taken from you?'

'Yes.'

And he had asked what was troubling her. Effie was over-whelmed by trouble.

'If we stay here, for a little while longer, until after the funeral, we'll keep out of your way.'

'If that's what you want, Effie.'

He was tempted to say that he didn't want her to keep out of his way, but she was right, they must keep a safe distance between them.

Eleven

HE WAS in the small room downstairs that he called his study, when there was a knock on the door, two knocks, the second one more like a bang.

It was Morag and Eddie, she shy, he cocky. He had done the banging. He now did the talking.

'Effie says can we have the kitchen. We're going to eat.'

'Tell her she can have the kitchen for as long as she likes. Tell her too there are some things in the fridge that I brought for you.'

'For me?'

'For you all.'

'What things?'

'Strawberry tarts.'

'Oh good, I like strawberry tarts.'

He rushed off. He did not use the main staircase, though it was closer. He had been given his instructions.

'He's not got very good manners,' said Morag, earnestly. 'He's just excited. I want to tell you, Mr Hamilton, that it wasn't Effie's fault that we weren't at the cinema to meet you. It was mine. I was too tired. Effie's going to take us to the pictures next Saturday. It's her birthday. She'll be twenty.'

He kept forgetting that Effie was so young.

Evidently he wasn't going to be included in the visit to the cinema.

'After we eat we're going to have a wee ceilidh. Effie's going to play her accordion. It's a very old one but she's a good player and she's never even had a lesson.'

'What are *you* going to do at the ceilidh?'

'I do a Highland dance.'

'I would like to see that.'

She didn't notice the hint.

'Did you have a nice time shopping?'

'Yes, thank you. Effie bought a new outfit. For the funeral. It's black. The lady in the shop said black suited her. So it does. She bought new underclothes too. She loves new underclothes.'

'What about you? Did you buy anything?'

'Yes. A dress. It's blue. Effie says it goes with my eyes. But if you'll excuse me, Mr Hamilton, I'd better go. Effie wants me to help her in the kitchen.'

He himself would have liked to go and help Effie in the kitchen.

He waited, in vain, for a belated invitation to Effie's birthday.

Later, he heard the accordion. He wasn't surprised that Effie preferred sad Gaelic airs. Once she sang, a lament, in Gaelic. He stood at the foot of the stairs, listening, moved to tears.

Twelve

MRS WILLIAMSON spent most of her time at the bedroom window, looking out for Daniel's motor caravan.

She must have a serious talk with Effie before he came.

So, after the children were asleep, she crept into Effie's room and found her, for the third time at least, trying on her new clothes.

Mrs Williamson ought to have been proud to have so beautiful and so superior a daughter, and so she would have been, if Effie hadn't been a rival whom Daniel would be sure to prefer.

It was true Effie didn't want him, but her aversion could be overcome if he could convince her that, when they were married, she could have Morag and Eddie to live with them. He had made promises but she did not think he would keep them. He might accept Morag, to begin with anyway, but he would refuse to take Eddie, for whom he had never shown any affection.

'It's Daniel, Effie. If he's going to marry one of us it ought to be me but I don't want to stand in your way. You did tell him you would think about it.'

Yes, there had been times when Effie had resolutely imagined Daniel doing to her what husbands did to wives. But that was long before she had met Gavin Hamilton.

'I don't want to marry him. I've made up my mind.'

'What about the children? Are you prepared to risk losing them?'

Effie stared at herself in the looking-glass. She saw a traitress, appropriately dressed in black, willing to sacrifice people she loved to save herself.

'Yes. Whatever happens I won't marry him. He should have married you years ago.'

'You won't mind then if I go off with him?'

'No.'

'That's settled then.'

Mrs Williamson got up and went over to the door, very quietly so as not to disturb Morag who was asleep.

'Effie?'

'Yes?'

'About you and Hamilton. I'm curious.'

'What do you mean?'

'He's taken a liking to you and you to him. Don't deny it.'

'He doesn't like me. He's just sorry for me.'

'Maybe you're right. But if it was me in your place I wouldn't be sleeping up here with my little sister. I'd be sleeping downstairs with him. But then I've always been more generous about loving than you. I never was one for keeping myself pure for the man I would marry. Hamilton will never marry you, pet, he'll marry some lady-body that's been to college, but you and him could have some happy times together. Well, good-night.'

Effie watched her mother leave in the looking-glass.

Thirteen

HE HAD said that he would be leaving the house early on Sunday. He had to pick up two elderly ladies and take them to the church. They lived twenty miles away up a remote glen.

Effie lay in bed, listening for the car and thinking about what her mother had said about her and Gavin. She had fallen asleep thinking about it.

He might not be in love with her but he was certainly attracted to her. She might not worship the ground he walked on but she felt very grateful to him, which was next door to loving him. Why then should she conspire to avoid him? He did not seem so intent on avoiding her. They would not sleep together; that, if it ever happened at all would be in the future, after they were married or at least engaged. Her mother had said that marriage was impossible, he would marry a lady-body who had been to college. But Effie in her new outfit could pass for a lady-body, and a teacher had once told her that she was clever enough to have gone to college, had things been different. She knew she had qualities that, if cultivated, would make her a wife fit for any man, even for a minister. All she needed was a little help and encouragement.

She had once before escaped the travelling life. When she was seventeen she had run away and found a job in

Inverness looking after a doctor's four children. She had done it well. They had been very pleased with her. Their friends were amazed when told she had been a traveller. Then she had met a young man, studying to be a teacher. His name was Donald Robertson. They had gone out together several times before his mother had found out and forbade him to see her any more. She had been greatly disappointed. She remembered weeping inconsolably. But what had forced her back to the travelling life was her concern for Morag and Eddie. She had heard that they were being badly neglected and were in danger of being taken into care. She had had to go back for them.

It could be different this time. She had been too young then. Gavin was a good bit older than Donald and had no mother to give him orders; indeed, he seemed to have no family at all. Above all he was genuinely fond of Morag and Eddie, and they of him. Donald hadn't known that they existed.

By nature she was not afraid to take risks, so why was she keeping out of his way when with a little boldness on her part they could be enjoying each other's company?

He would become a minister in four years. In half that time she could learn to be a minister's wife. In the meantime she would meet his friends and hold her head high.

In the end she might not succeed. They would go their separate ways and never see each other again. But she could have improved herself so much that she might meet some other good man who would marry her and adopt Morag and Eddie as his own.

She heard the car. Quickly she got out of bed and ran across to the window to catch a glimpse of it before it disappeared among the trees.

She hurried back to bed, happier and more confident than she had felt for a long time.

Morag was still half asleep. 'What's the matter?' she asked.

Effie tickled her. 'Nothing's the matter. Nothing in the world. Everything's fine. Everything's wonderful.'

Morag was delighted. Effie was once again the big sister who joked with them and made them laugh, no longer the worried guardian who scolded them.

'It's going to be a lovely day,' said Effie. 'We'll go and build sandcastles.'

'Will we be allowed, Effie?'

'Who's going to stop us?'

Eddie, the forager, had found in a cupboard buckets and spades and a big football.

After a shower, her sixth she thought but she had lost count, she put on her red dress and went downstairs to the kitchen, where the first thing she did was put on an apron, Gavin's, and the second thing was to notice a sheet of paper on the table, with writing on it.

She was sure it hadn't been there last night. It must be a message from Gavin.

She was afraid that she might not be able to understand it. She could read print well enough, but she had little experience of reading scribbled longhand. She was also afraid that it might be to tell her that he wanted them all out of his house by the time he came home.

Morag came into the kitchen. She saw the sheet of paper in Effie's hand.

'What's that?' she asked, cheerfully.

'I think it's a message from Gavin.'

'What does it say?'

'I haven't read it yet.'

'Read it now.'

'You read it.'

Morag took the paper and carefully deciphered it.

'"Won't be home till three. Remember the McTeagues are visiting you this afternoon."'

'Does it really say visiting us?'

'Yes. Who are the McTeagues?'

'Mr McTeague is the head man in the forest.'

'I thought Mr Hamilton was the head man.'

'He's not really a forestry worker. He's going to be a minister.'

'In a church?'

'Yes.'

'Will he have to go to college?'

'Yes.'

'When?'

'I think he said October.'

Morag counted the months on her fingers. 'July, August, September, October. What will we do then?'

'I expect we'll be long gone by then.'

They set the table, using Hamilton's china delftware and steel cutlery. He had given permission. Make yourselves at home, he had said.

They had never really had a home. You couldn't call a temporary campsite home.

'Are you friends with Mr Hamilton now, Effie?' Morag asked.

'I hope so, love.'

'The children look half-starved, Effie,' he had said. 'Feed them well.'

So it was the best breakfast Eddie had ever had: porridge, ham and eggs, toast, and milk to drink. He ate everything.

Morag had to be coaxed to eat. She had little appetite.

'If she doesn't perk up, we'll have to take her to a doctor,' Gavin had said.

Effie's greatest concern was that Morag might become dangerously ill.

It seemed that Gavin was anxious too.

It brought them close.

After making sure that the kitchen was as tidy as they could make it, they set off for the sands, Morag in her new blue dress with a blue ribbon in her hair, Eddie in his smart new shorts and new red jersey with a white collar, and Effie in her red dress; underneath it she wore her black swimming costume. She loved swimming.

Mrs Williamson had been invited but she preferred to stay in the house, to look after her father, she said, but really to sit by the window, looking out for Daniel.

Eddie was carrying the ball, Morag the bucket and spade.

At the gate they met a family: father and mother, a girl, and a boy. The girl, about Morag's age, had a dog on a lead.

'Do you live here?' asked the woman. She was English.

'Yes,' said Effie.

'Is it all right if we go in and have a look?'

Effie spoke primly. 'Yes, but please don't forget to shut the gate. The horses might wander onto the road.'

It wasn't likely. The two old horses were enjoying the rest and the lush grass.

'This is the Old Manse, isn't it?' said the woman.

'Yes.'

'There's a rose garden, we were told. Visitors are welcome, aren't they?'

'Yes.'

'Thank you. We'll keep Judy on her leash.'

Effie and the children went on towards the sands.

'Do we really live here, Effie?' asked Morag.

'We slept here last night, didn't we? We're going to sleep here tonight. So of course we live here.'

'Yes, but I think they thought the house was ours.'

There were already several families on the sands.

Effie and the children were observed with interest, because they were speaking Gaelic and because Effie with her happy laughter was very attractive.

As enthusiastic as a child herself she played football with Eddie, helped Morag to build a sandcastle, and raced them both, giving them big head starts, and letting Eddie win.

People laughed at how gleeful the little boy was at his victory.

'Do you know what I'm going to do?' said Effie.

They waited, eagerly. Effie often gave them surprises.

'Do you see that little island?'

It was about a quarter of a mile offshore.

'I'm going to swim to it.'

Morag was doubtful. 'It's too far, Effie.'

'Effie's swum further than that,' said Eddie.

'You don't have to do it,' said Morag.

'Yes, pet, I do.'

Even as a child Effie had felt compelled to set herself tests.

Morag was puzzled. 'Why do you have to?'

'I'll tell you later.' Years later, perhaps.

Effie took off her dress and then, in her black swimming costume, ran into the water. She would have to wade a good fifty yards before it was deep enough for her to dive in.

'Can you speak English?' asked a man nearby. 'What's your sister doing?'

'She's swimming to the island.' Morag pointed.

'Will she be all right? Has she done it before?'

'No.'

'She'll be all right,' said the man's wife. 'She's a big strong girl.'

Effie was pretending that Gavin Hamilton was on the island, waiting for her.

Fourteen

HAMILTON WAS thinking hard about his relationship with Effie and her family.

He was reluctant to call his offering them the use of his field a mistake; it had been necessary, an act of humanity; but perhaps his inviting them into his house had been impulsive and over-zealous. He had not taken time to consider their feelings. Effie's accusation that he was trying to take away what pride they had left had been unfair, but from her point of view it was justified. She had realised the price that they, she especially, would have to pay when, inevitably, after only a few days of spacious rooms and high ceilings, they would have to go back to crawling in and out of low, grimy tents. Moreover, he had in front of him the invidious task of telling them they had to leave. He might have to get Sheila McTeague to do it for him. She would take Effie aside and explain the situation. Effie wasn't stupid; she would understand. She was proud too and wouldn't want to stay where she wasn't wanted or rather where she knew there could be no place for her.

He was not sure what the effect of their being sent away would have on him. He was already fond of the two children and they of him. As for Effie he not only had respect for her, he also felt some affection.

The affair of the tramp and the pay packet should have

been a lesson to him. There was no virtue in being kind to people if in doing so you humiliated them. He would never forget the old tramp weeping and yelling abuse at him.

He hoped he would not have similar memories of Effie.

'What you need, Gavin,' Sheila McTeague had said, tartly, 'is a wife like Fiona McDonald. She would see to it you didn't take your Christianity too seriously.'

Daughter of a minister, niece of a moderator, and sister of a minister, Fiona had been brought up to look upon undue zeal as no better than bad manners. Respectability and good sense were the hallmarks of a Christian gentleman. Christians had to be charitable but only to those who deserved it and would appreciate it. If Gavin wanted to succeed as a minister he would do well to heed Fiona's advice. He had once confessed to Sheila and Hugh that it was his ambition to take part in, perhaps to lead, a crusade to convert the Church of Scotland into a pacifist organisation, as it ought to be. Fiona's cold common sense would quickly quench that particular passion.

Though he was never seen to offer her any encouragement it was assumed by most of the congregation that she would have him in the end. That she was ten years older than he, had no figure to speak of, and was very prudish, would not matter; it would be the least physical of marriages.

To those sceptical about such a marriage ever taking place it was pointed out that Miss Fiona must love him in her own peculiar way, and as for Hamilton he was well aware of the advantages of marrying her. Not only did she have influential church connections, she had also been left a good deal of money.

Fifteen

SHEILA MCTEAGUE had not gone to church that morning. She had been busy looking out cast-off clothing. It amounted to a goodly bundle: dresses for the little girl, shorts and shirts for the little boy, slacks, blouses and underwear for the young woman.

Hugh looked on, with a frown.

'You think I should give them to the charity shop?' she asked.

'No, but you will have to be careful not to hurt their feelings, especially the young woman's.'

'Heavens, Hugh, she's just a tinker girl. Don't they scrounge and beg their way through life?'

'No, they do not. They work very hard. That girl has got more pride and self-respect than many a titled lady.'

Sheila had to laugh. 'Don't exaggerate. How many titled ladies do you know?'

'You're going to get a surprise when you meet her.'

'You're making me jealous!'

In the car Sheila gave some last instructions to her own two children.

'Remember these people haven't been as fortunate as we have. They don't live in houses. They live in tents. They're very poor. They start work as soon as they can walk.'

'What kind of work?' asked Ian.

'They fish for pearls in ice-cold rivers. They lift potatoes in frosty fields. They help at harvest time.'

'Why have they come here? There aren't any pearls in the Kilcalmonell burn.'

'There's an old man who's dying. His family were buried here eighty years ago. He wants to be buried beside them.'

'Are they foreigners?'

'No, they're Scottish, like us. They speak Gaelic; well, a kind of Gaelic.'

'Can they speak English?'

'I think so. Yes.'

Deirdre so far had said nothing. It wouldn't matter to her if the tinkers were poor and dirty. She had other criteria.

They arrived at the Old Manse gate.

Sheila got out and opened it. She heard a little boy screaming. It was a high-pitched, happy scream.

He was playing football with his big sister in the field behind the house. Effie was running about with the natural grace that had so impressed Hugh and the men at the hut.

The McTeagues got out of the car.

'I see what you mean, Hugh,' whispered Sheila. 'She's quite beautiful.'

Effie came running to greet them. 'Hello. Gavin's not back yet. I don't think he'll be long. I'm Effie. This is Morag, and this is Eddie.'

'I'm Sheila and this is my husband Hugh. I think you've already met. This is Deirdre and this is Ian.'

'My mother's upstairs keeping my grandfather company.'

'How is he?'

'He's very ill.'

'Shouldn't he be in hospital?'

'He doesn't want to die in a hospital.'

Suddenly Deirdre went forward without a word and embraced Effie.

Effie was a little embarrassed but very pleased.

Sheila felt very proud of her ten-year-old daughter.

Here was no sluttish, scheming would-be seducer. In that respect this girl was as innocent as Gavin. Her eyes were the colour of beech leaves in autumn. They were honest and intelligent.

Did Gavin realise what a treasure he had here?

There was the merest hint of coarseness, which was no wonder, considering the harshness of her life.

They heard a car coming up to the house. It was Hamilton's. He parked it alongside the McTeagues'. He got out with an eagerness not quite in keeping with his Sunday suit.

He went straight to Effie. 'Sorry I'm a bit late. Did you have lunch?'

'Yes, thank you.'

'Effie swam to the island,' said Eddie, proudly.

'What island?' asked Hamilton, alarmed.

Eddie pointed. 'They all clapped.'

'There are dangerous currents in the loch,' said Hamilton, 'and it's a good half mile there and back. What possessed you, Effie?'

She laughed. 'Maybe, one day, I'll tell you.'

She had already found the right attitude to adopt towards him: that of a younger sister, frank, friendly, humorous, a wee bit cheeky, and with absolutely no sexual allure.

He was still trying to find a satisfactory attitude to her.

Towards the two children he was like an affectionate uncle.

Sheila had never liked him more than she did now. There was not a trace of his exasperating self-righteousness.

'Would you like tea?' asked Effie. 'I've set the table in the big room.'

Sheila was amused. Good for you, Effie, she thought. Previously when she and Hugh had tea with Gavin it had been in the kitchen. The big room with its expensive furniture was reserved for visitors like Fiona McDonald.

'You don't mind, Gavin?' said Effie.

'Of course not.'

Fiona and her friends would have been shocked at what they would have called the impudence of the girl. They would have refused her naive hospitality as hurtfully as they could.

'It's just fairy cakes and biscuits,' said Effie.

The big round mahogany table had a white cloth spread over it. The dishes were Gavin's bone china, which had come from the Big House.

Effie had probably never drunk out of a bone-china cup in her life. Bashed tinnies would have been what she was accustomed to.

It occurred to Sheila that though Effie was laughing and apparently enjoying her role as hostess it must be a great strain and she would suffer for it later.

Eddie had an opinion to express. He did it boldly, with his mouth full of fairy cake.

'Mr Hamilton's the second best person in the world. Effie's the best.'

'You're a wee blether,' said Effie.

When tea was over Sheila asked Hugh to bring in the suitcase containing the clothes. It was her turn to be under a strain. She would never forgive herself if she caused this girl any distress.

Hugh put the suitcase on the kitchen table.

'Now you two go for a walk,' she said.

She opened the suitcase. 'These are some clothes we've grown out of. These trousers,' – she held them up – 'are too tight for me now.'

'Thank you very much, Mrs McTeague,' said Effie.

'Please call me Sheila.'

Effie smiled but wasn't sure.

Eddie, in a smart-looking jacket, strutted about importantly. Morag had picked up a dress, red with white dots.

'Say thank you to Mrs McTeague,' said Effie.

Eddie said it cockily, Morag shyly.

Ian thought he might have left something in a pocket of the jacket. 'Maybe a marble.'

'You're being stupid, Ian,' said Deirdre.

Eddie searched all the pockets. 'There's nothing.'

What could have been awkward had been made easy by the two small boys.

'I'd like to give you something,' said Effie.

'There's no need, Effie.'

How could people so poor have anything to give?

'I won't be a minute.'

Effie hurried out and was soon back, with the Oxo cube tin in her hand.

Sheila wondered what it could be, and prepared herself to give thanks for some cheap trinket Effie had found in exchange for her hand-me-downs.

She opened the tin, drew breath. Deirdre clamoured for her to lower the tin so she too could see what was inside.

'Oh, Effie. They're beautiful. Simply wonderful.' Two

perfect little pearls sat side by side in the tin, held in place by a small piece of gold thread.

Sheila looked at Deirdre and knew she would already be planning a necklace or a bracelet for each of them, determining exactly what kind of chain each little pearl would be hung on. Well, why not, she thought, and looked at Effie and the children in delight.

Sixteen

EFFIE AND Hamilton were having a quiet moment in the kitchen together. The McTeagues had left, and Effie felt she had had a small victory there. She was proud of the children too. They had got along so well with Deirdre and Ian. She felt sure she had seen the beginnings of real friendship between them.

She was about to explain to Hamilton how happy and relieved she felt, when her mother came into the kitchen, greeted them briefly and told Hamilton that her father wanted to see him.

Hamilton was feeling a little guilty that he hadn't already made an effort to see the sick, lonely old man.

'You too, Effie.'

'I don't want to see him.'

Hamilton was surprised by Effie's bitterness.

'He wants to make me promise to marry Daniel Stewart.'

'Why should he want you to marry a man nearly thirty years older than you?'

'Because Daniel paid him.'

'Now, Effie,' said her mother, 'you know that's not why. You see, Mr Hamilton, Grandfather's anxious that Effie stays one of us. She's already run away once.'

'And I'll run away again.'

'If she was to marry Daniel she'd have to stay, especially if she had a child by him.'

Effie clutched Hamilton's arm. 'I want to tell you something.'

'For Christ's sake, Effie,' cried her mother, 'it's family business and it happened long ago. Mr Hamilton's not interested.'

But Hamilton was interested. 'What is it, Effie?'

'On my fifteenth birthday they tried to trick me into marrying him. They didn't tell me he was already married to a woman who'd run away from him. I think I was drugged. There was a kind of ceremony. They gave me a ring. They said I was married and I had to let him sleep with me. They brought him, my mother and my grandfather and two of their cronies, brought him to my tent in the middle of the night when I was asleep.'

'God forgive us,' cried her mother, 'we were all drunk.'

'They tore off my clothes. They tried to help him to rape me.'

'Rape? Christ, Effie, how could it be rape? We did it because we loved you, because we wanted you to be one of us.'

Effie burst into tears. She clutched Hamilton's arm. With her other hand she hid her face.

'What's all the fuss about?' cried her mother. 'No harm was done. He couldn't get near her. She was like a young tiger, scratching, and biting. I got a kick in the face. She's always wanted, God knows why, to keep herself pure for the man she marries. It's not such a precious thing, is it? If I had been like her she wouldn't be here. Her father was a ploughboy in Ross-shire. He couldn't have been any more than sixteen. I was even younger. He liked me, I liked him, he wanted it, so I let him have it. In a byre, among the beasts. I heard he was killed in the War.'

Then, when Mrs Williamson, and Effie herself, were expecting Hamilton to go off in disgust, he took Effie in his arms and held her tight. 'Dear Effie.'

'I felt dirty then and I still feel dirty. No decent man will even want to marry me.' With a cry of despair and anguish she struggled out of his arms and rushed out of the room.

'She's always been too sensitive for her own good. Anyway, Daniel's not coming to marry her. He's coming to marry me. He just doesn't know it yet.'

Seventeen

HE THOUGHT he would find her hiding somewhere, breaking her heart and being sorry for herself. He wouldn't blame her.

It showed how much he had to learn about her. She had to be courageous not only for her own sake but for the children's too. If she ever gave in God knew what would happen to them.

There she was, at the burn, helping Eddie to catch minnows in a tin saucepan. He was not having much success.

Hamilton went over. 'You'll never catch them that way.'

'Show us how,' said Effie.

'Yes, show us,' cried Eddie.

There were still marks of tears on her face but she was smiling.

'We'll need two jam jars, clear glass, a piece of string, and a long stick. I've some jam jars in the cupboard under the sink and string in a drawer in the kitchen. I'll go and get them.'

'No, I'll get them.' Effie ran off.

There were plenty of sticks lying around. Eddie gathered at least six.

Morag came up to Hamilton. 'Why was Effie crying? Eddie and me don't like it when she cries. We get frightened. Nobody wants us, except her.'

'Your mother wants you.'

'She thinks we're nuisances.'

'Well, I want you.'

She looked at him doubtfully. She meant, you're very nice, but you're a stranger, you don't come into it, you have no say.

Whatever happens, he thought, I can't let this little girl down.

Effie came back, with the jam jars and the string.

They watched as Hamilton tied the string round the neck of one of the jars. Then he lowered it cautiously into a pool, so that it lay on its side, with the mouth facing upstream. Soon minnows came to have a look.

With the stick he gently steered a minnow into the jar. It went in but darted out again. He tried again, and again.

Eddie was impatient to try.

They were talking in whispers, so as not to alarm the tiny fish.

A minnow ventured into the jar. Hamilton instantly lifted the jar by the string. There was the captive, looking disgusted with itself.

It was Eddie's turn.

At first he was in too big a hurry and the minnows all escaped but soon, with Effie's tactful assistance, he got one. 'It's the biggest,' he cried. Soon he had caught four more.

All the captives were put in the second jar.

'What do we do with them now?' asked Eddie. 'They're too wee to eat.'

'And they'll die if they're kept in the jar,' said Hamilton. 'Why not put them back in the burn? It's catching them that's the fun.'

At first Eddie was shocked at the very idea.

'You could always catch more.'

'Do you want me to let them go?'

'Yes. They're happier in the burn with their friends.'

'All right.'

With the air of one making a painful but noble sacrifice Eddie emptied the jar into the burn. The minnows darted off.

'Well done, Eddie,' said Hamilton. 'Look, they're telling one another about the little boy who set them free.'

Eddie grinned. 'They can't speak.'

Hamilton noticed Effie giving him a curious look.

'He would never have done that for anyone but you.'

'Can we go now and gather roses?' asked Morag.

They went off to gather roses.

Eighteen

THAT NIGHT Mrs Williamson came again into Effie's room. She sat on the bed where Morag was sound asleep.

In her nightgown Effie was at the window, looking at the moon shining on the loch. It was shining in the room too.

They whispered in Gaelic.

'I've seen the moon shining on water hundreds of times,' said Effie, 'but this is the first time I've realised how beautiful it is.'

'You've had a great weight taken off your mind, and you couldn't say, could you, that beautiful things have come into our lives very much?'

'No.'

'I shouldn't have said that about your father. But I was bonny too when I was young and I had to have my own ways of finding enjoyment.'

'I'm not judging you, mother.'

'The last thing I want is to spoil things for you. He likes you, Effie.'

'He's sorry for me, that's all.'

'It's a lot more than that, and it will grow. If you were to stay here for a month or two, who knows what might happen? Aren't there stories of traveller girls marrying rich men, men with titles even?'

There were such stories.

'He's not the kind who after he'd talked you into his bed would throw you away like a dirty clout.'

'He would never try to talk me into his bed.'

'Maybe not. Maybe he's like you, the whole thing or nothing. You could break each other's hearts. The trouble is, Effie, if he married you you'd get everything, he'd get nothing.'

When her mother was gone Effie went and looked at herself in a mirror on the wall. Last night she had seen a self-piteous, woebegone face. Now she was seeing a girl with an unflinching gaze and her head held high.

'He wouldn't be getting nothing,' she said. 'He'd be getting me, Effie Williamson.'

Nineteen

BACK TO her role of younger sister, Effie did not go down to the kitchen to help him prepare his sandwiches and fill his thermos flask with tea.

He had told her that on work days he left the house at half-past seven in the morning and came home at six in the evening. She lay and listened. She did not hear much for he was being deliberately quiet so as not to disturb anyone.

She smelled reek, peat reek. He must have lit a fire in the big room.

Rain pattered against the window.

It was incredible enough that he had let them into his house, now he was giving himself a great deal of trouble making it comfortable for them.

Why was he doing it? Again she hurried away from that question.

All the same, even if it was the most unlikely thing in the world that he would ever ask her to marry him, she would still try to make herself worthy of him.

When she was sure, from the silence below, that he had gone she got up and took a shower, using scented soap. Her period was almost over. She washed herself thoroughly. She brushed her hair until it shone. She put on clean under-clothes and the fawn slacks that Mrs McTeague had given her; they went well with her blue blouse.

In Towellan she had daringly bought lipstick. Now she put a little on.

Morag was gazing at her solemnly from the bed. Now and then she coughed.

'How do I look?' asked Effie, turning round and round.

'You look very nice.'

'So will you, pet, when you put on the dress with white dots.'

'I'm too thin.'

'You'll have to eat more and become fat.'

'Are you happy, Effie?'

'Yes, but I'll be a lot happier when you've got rid of that cough. The doctor will give you something for it.'

'Mother said we'd have to leave the house when grandfather died. I saw him yesterday and I thought he was dead already.'

'Maybe Mr Hamilton will let us stay a bit longer.'

'When we leave where will we go? I don't want to sleep in a tent again.'

'You won't have to. We'll find a place.'

'Eddie says he'll run away and hide in the trees.'

Hamilton had said that he would arrange for the doctor to call that morning.

In the big room the fire was blazing. There was a brass scuttle full of coal and a wicker basket with peats in it. The room was pleasantly warm.

She remembered many mornings when she had crawled out of the tent into the rain, shivering and miserable, having to make a great effort to get a fire going.

No wonder Morag was not well.

On the table was a box containing children's games, like

ludo and snakes-and-ladders. He must have looked them out for Morag and Eddie.

For years she had had to carry so many burdens. Now they had been removed, as if by magic, even if it was only for a little while. Someone else was carrying them for her. It was too wonderful to be true, and yet it was true.

Would he have done all this out of pity? Yes, he would. He was that kind of man.

Suddenly she felt a great fear, not on her own account but his. In her experience she had found that goodness and generosity were often not rewarded as they should be. Suppose, that morning, at his work, there was an accident, a tree fell and killed him.

To drive that awful vision from her mind she embraced Eddie, to his astonishment. He had asked for another slice of toast and was being kissed.

'Is anything the matter, Effie?' asked Morag.

'No, pet, nothing's the matter. Finish your porridge.'

Effie took some breakfast up to her mother.

She found her in grandfather's room. He seemed to be asleep. He looked dead.

'It won't be long now,' said her mother. 'Do you know what he wants? He wants to die in a tent. God knows why.'

But Effie knew. He had been a tent-dweller all his long life, and his ancestors before him, for hundreds of years. They had never been ashamed of it, and now, when he was dying, his life coming to an end, he wished to honour it.

'What are we going to do, Effie?'

'We'll put up a tent and try to be ready.'

'You're a good girl, Effie.'

Effie stood looking down at the old man's face, ravaged by age and pain, but still with traces of dignity and authority clinging to it. A university professor had said that if he had been born into another sphere of life he would have been a great and famous man.

She had good reason to distrust him. If she had obeyed him she would have been very unhappily married to Daniel Stewart and her life ruined, but she was grateful to him too. It must have been from him that she had inherited the unshakeable conviction that she was somehow special.

Twenty

THEY WERE in the big room, Effie in an armchair trying to read a book, with the aid of a dictionary, and Morag and Eddie lying on the carpet playing ludo, when they heard a car arriving. It did not go round to the back of the house as other cars did but stopped outside the front door.

Effie thought it was the doctor but when she went to the window she saw that it was a woman, smartly dressed in a dark-blue outfit with hat to match, and carrying what looked like a book.

The doorbell rang. Effie hurried to answer it, but before she got there the door, or rather the two doors, the outer and the inner, burst open and the visitor came stamping angrily into the hall.

She glared haughtily at Effie. 'Who are you? What were you doing in that room?'

While Effie was wondering how to react to this uncalled-for rudeness the visitor gave another exhibition of it.

'I hope you realise you've no right to be in this house?'

The reason why Miss Fiona was so rude, she who had been brought up to be civil, even to servants, was because she was in a state of shock. She had come expecting to see a coarse, slovenly girl, and here she was confronted by a scrupulously clean, politely smiling, obviously intelligent, young woman – very good-looking too – with an enviable figure.

Miss Fiona felt that she was the victim of some trickery.

'Do you know who I am?' she cried. Even to herself it sounded petty.

'I'm afraid I don't,' said Effie.

'I'm a very close friend of Mr Hamilton.' She almost added that they were engaged, but it would have been too blatant a lie.

'Mr Hamilton's at work,' said Effie. 'He won't be home till six o'clock. Would you like me to tell him you called?'

Miss Fiona then remembered that she had come armed. It wasn't a book she was holding but a magazine. It contained pictures of travellers, showing them to be miserable, dirty, ragged subhuman creatures. How then to see this elegant young woman as one of them? Again Miss Fiona suspected trickery.

'Would you please see that Mr Hamilton gets this?'

She handed the magazine to Effie.

'You may find it interesting yourself, particularly pages 26, 27 and 28.'

As Effie turned the glossy pages she had already guessed what it was she was being asked to look at. This was a magazine that catered for well-to-do people who lived in the country in big houses and who were prepared to tolerate the travellers as a quaint feature of the countryside as long as their encampments were too far off to be seen, heard, or smelled. They brought their guests in big expensive cars or on horseback to have a look at them.

'Do you recognise any of your friends?' asked Miss McDonald.

Her expectation had been that Effie would cringe in shame, but the result could not have been more different.

Effie could hardly feel proud of these unfortunate tribespeople of hers, so utterly poor, so unavoidably squalid, but she felt what was more important, what gave her the strength of mind to reject this stupid woman's scorn and contempt. She felt affection, and thought that if she had to go back and live among them again she would do it with resolution and spend the rest of her life trying to improve their conditions.

Yes, she did recognise one or two. She had been a guest in those shabby, leaking, smelly tents. She had sat in sunshine outside them drinking tea and gossiping. She had held those babies in her arms. She had given swimming lessons to those ragged children. She had nursed those old women with their seamed, pain-stricken faces.

If they could have seen her now, so well-dressed, so comfortable in this fine big house they would have been amazed but they would also have been pleased for her. They had often assured her that she would not remain a traveller all her days, she was too clever, too brave, too beautiful.

'Why do you want Mr Hamilton to see these pictures?' she asked. 'Is it so that he will think badly of me?'

Miss McDonald was disappointed with herself. She had come intending to show an example of civilised behaviour, sympathetic but frank and firm. Instead she was being mean and unfair. The reason was humiliating; she was jealous of this young woman.

'You really shouldn't be in this house,' she said, trying to sound reasonable.

'Mr Hamilton invited us.'

Miss McDonald looked into the big room, expecting to find mess and damage. What she saw were two children lying on the floor, their game of ludo suspended. They were watching her with curiosity, as if puzzled that someone so well-dressed should behave so poorly.

The little girl looked to be in the early stages of consumption. It was rife in the camps. It had said so in the magazine.

'I'm sorry,' said Miss McDonald, and hurried out to her car. She did not immediately drive off.

She had meant well but bringing the magazine had been a bad mistake. Seeing those pictures Gavin might well be disgusted, but not with the people in them.

Twenty-one

THE DOCTOR'S car passed Miss McDonald's on the drive. He gave her a smile and a wave but she was too preoccupied with her thoughts to notice. Had she come, as the minister's sister, to offer her help to these outcasts who had come into the parish? He hoped so but doubted it.

He was met at the back door by as attractive a young woman as he had seen in a long time; not just attractive, but intelligent and mannerly.

'I'm Effie,' she said, 'Effie Williamson. Morag's sister.'

'I'm Doctor Baxter.'

He had noticed immediately that in spite of her brave smiles she was under a great strain, and had been for years. You didn't come from origins like hers, and lead the kind of life she had, without having had to endure a great deal. He felt moved by her lack of self-pity; she had plenty of self-respect, but not a trace of self-pity. He was greatly taken with Miss Effie Williamson.

She took him through to the big room.

The two children got to their feet. Not only was she well-mannered herself, she was training the children to be well-mannered too.

'Hello, children,' he said, 'I see you've been playing ludo. Who won?'

'It's not finished yet,' said the little girl, earnestly. 'But Eddie's got more men home.'

'I threw lots of sixes,' said Eddie, modestly.

Dr Baxter had played ludo often when his own children were young.

'Well, young lady, let me have a look at you.'

He lifted Morag onto a chair and sounded her with his stethoscope.

Effie watched anxiously. 'She's got a bad cough, doctor.'

He had been afraid of tuberculosis. 'We'll soon get rid of that.'

What he wanted to prescribe not only for her but for the little boy too, and for the young woman, was at least a month in this comfortable house, with a proper bed to sleep in, good food to eat, and plenty of fresh air.

He would have a word with Gavin.

'It's not TB, is it?' whispered Effie.

'No, but we'll have to be careful. How are you keeping yourself, Effie?'

'Oh, I'm fine. I'm never ill.'

If she was she'd never admit it. The children depended on her. That was a good part of the trouble.

'I hear you're pearl-fishers.'

'Not any longer, I think. The mussels are getting very scarce.'

'I believe your mother and grandfather are with you?'

'Yes. Grandfather's very ill but he won't go into hospital.'

'I understand. Well, I'll send something for the cough by Willie the Bus, and a tonic. I'll leave a note for Gavin. Tell him I'll call in tomorrow evening and have a chat with him. In the meantime, young lady, you take it easy.'

He scribbled a note for Gavin.

She saw him to the door.

'How are you getting on with Gavin?'

He thought she blushed, but she was too tanned to tell.

'All right. He's very kind. He's fond of the children.'

And he's a fool, thought the doctor, if he doesn't become fond of you.

Twenty-two

On Monday morning Hamilton's workmates were keen to hear how he had got on with the 'tinks'. They had heard that he had let them into his house. Surely it couldn't be true? You might as well invite a bunch of cattle; the beasts would be no less house-trained. It was bad enough, having a death in your family, with all the fuss with doctors and undertakers, but it would be a lot worse if the deceased was a complete stranger, and a scruffy one at that. What did the young woman look like, after she'd had a good wash? That was, if she had had a good wash. Weren't her kind happier when dirty?

Hamilton let them talk and joke. Effie was a secret he was not going to share with anyone.

The rain had gone off. It was now warm and sunny. Their task was to cut away the bracken that was threatening to smother a whole area of recently planted trees.

They worked side by side.

Hamilton became aware that the man on his right had changed. It had been Ian McPhee, it was now Hamish McKenzie.

Ian was a taciturn fellow, who grunted oftener than he spoke. Hamish usually didn't even grunt.

At twenty-one Hamish was the youngest man working in the forest, and the most powerfully built. He had to be kept in check by his mates. For instance, they thought six hundred trees were quite enough for a man to plant in a day. Hamish could easily manage twice that number, so he had to be restrained. He was far from bright but his cheerful good humour made up for it. He had difficulty first in finding a girlfriend and then in keeping her. One had complained it was like looking after a wean; a wean six feet tall and weighing a hundred and sixty pounds. All the same in some respects he could be considered quite a catch. He had a good job and would have it all his life. When he married he would be eligible for a forestry house. He had money in the bank, being a canny saver.

'Do you mind if I ask you something, Gavin?'

'Not at all, Hamish. What is it you want to ask me?'

'That girl you've got staying with you, the tinker girl, I'd like to meet her.'

Hamilton was dumbfounded.

'I saw her in Towellan on Saturday. She had two children with her. I wanted to talk to her but I thought I should wait till I was introduced. Do you know if she has a boyfriend in the place she came from?'

'I don't think so.'

'Do you think she would like to meet me?'

Well, thought Hamilton, would she? In several respects he would make her a suitable husband. His mother, big Elspeth, had once been in service and now worked in a dairy; his father, Stevie, was a labourer with a local builder's and drank too much. So they weren't all that much higher in the social scale. They were good-hearted and would welcome her into the family. He would be kind to her. She would manage his affairs better than he did himself. She might even strike a spark or two of intelligence from him. She would never have to go back to the travelling life.

'*You're* not her boyfriend, are you, Gavin?'

Hamilton did not know what to say. If he said no he would be telling the truth but not the whole truth, for she was his secret and nobody else's. If he said yes, he would be committing himself openly. He was not sure he wanted to do that. Hamish, not out of malice, but like a thwarted child, would want to tell everyone of his disappointment.

Suppose, thought Hamilton, suppose I let this well-meaning booby steal her from under my nose. Suppose I reconcile myself to her marrying him and having children by him, how would it affect me? Would I wish them well and then concentrate on my studies, with renewed zest?

He couldn't answer those questions.

Twenty-three

He was astonished and alarmed when he saw a tent, a tinker's bow-tent, erected on the field. He went over and lifted the entrance flap. There was no one in it but a bed had been made up. Had Effie gone back to her refusal to sleep in the house? He felt dismayed.

She had been on the lookout for him. She came out of the house.

'What's the tent for?' he asked.

'Grandfather doesn't want to die in the house. He says he was born in a tent and he wants to die in one.'

He smiled. 'Does it matter where you die?'

'Oh yes, it does.' She spoke with great earnestness.

'Suppose he dies in the middle of the night?'

'We'll try to be ready.'

He should remember that these people, Effie among them, were pagans. Owing to the way they lived they were bound to be closer to animal ways of thinking than those people who lived in houses and worshipped in churches.

Did not deer, when old and dying, creep off to some secret place of their own to wait for death?

'Did the doctor come?'

'Yes, he said he didn't think it was TB.'

'Thank God for that.'

'He left a note for you.'

She smiled. 'He seemed anxious about me. I told him I was never ill. Someone else called. Miss McDonald, she said.'

'What did she want?'

'She brought a magazine for you to see. It's got pictures of a travellers' camp.'

'Was she unpleasant?'

'Yes, but I think she was a wee bit ashamed of it.'

Later, in the kitchen, after he had eaten she handed him the magazine.

'I don't think I want to see it.'

'Pages 26, 27 and 28.'

He turned to those pages. He looked at the pictures for a minute or so.

She wondered what he was going to say.

'That little girl,' he said, 'could be Morag.'

'She could be me.'

He glanced at her. 'You've come a long way, Effie.'

It was a journey that must have taken great courage and determination. Perhaps one day she would tell him about it.

'I've got something to tell you,' he said.

She waited, smiling.

As fairly as he could he told her about Hamish. She asked no questions.

When he was finished she said, 'Why have you told me this?'

'I thought I had no right to keep you to myself.'

'But what if I want you to keep me to yourself?'

'Do you, Effie?'

'Yes.'

'What am I to tell Hamish?'

'Tell him that Miss Williamson thanks him but she's already spoken for.'

'I'll have great pleasure in telling him that.'

She went over to the sink where the dirty dishes waited.

'I'll wash, you dry.'

He had to smile. This was Effie, one minute as intimate as a wife, the next as aloof as a deer.

'This birthday celebration on Saturday? Am I invited?'

'I didn't think you'd want to come.'

'Of course I want to come.'

'Morag wants to invite the McTeague children.'

'What a good idea. They'll be delighted.'

'Will their mother let them come?'

'Don't worry. Sheila will be pleased that they've been invited. After the cinema are we to have a feast, well, high tea, at the Royal?'

'Is that the big hotel on the seafront?'

'Where all the best people hold their celebrations.'

'I thought we would go to a cafe.'

'Isn't this a special occasion, calling for waitress service and white tablecloths?'

'I've never been in a hotel like that before.'

He couldn't resist giving her a quick kiss on the cheek.

He shouldn't have, though. She blushed. This time it was very visible.

'Sorry, Effie.'

'It's all right.'

Later they went out to sit in the garden. Eddie was kicking a ball about in the field. Morag was gathering roses. Hamilton had asked her to. 'For Effie,' he had said. 'All the roses in the world are for Effie.'

Morag had smiled. This was one of the silly things grown-ups said, but it was meant as a compliment to Effie, so she approved of it.

'I don't think I've been in a more beautiful place,' said Effie. 'So peaceful. So safe.'

'Safe?'

'My mother keeps expecting the police to come and chase us all away. You too, Gavin. She can't understand how you came to own this big house.'

'Didn't you explain?'

'I tried to, but she's often afraid. It's not easy not to be afraid if you've got no rights and everywhere you go people don't want you and chase you off.'

'Are you afraid, Effie?'

'Sometimes.'

'Are you afraid now, sitting here, beside me?'

She shuddered, but tried to smile.

'Yes, but it's a different kind of fear.'

He decided not to ask what kind. He would find out later.

'Tell me, Effie, in traveller mythology, is there a story about a roe deer being turned into a beautiful girl?'

'There could be. We have lots of stories about animals. We live close to them. Why do you ask?'

'Because it's the only way to account for your amazing elegance.'

'Have I got amazing elegance?'

'Even Angus noticed it. And you can run faster than Eddie.'

'I can't run faster than you.'

There had been a race. Hamilton had won.

'You can swim for miles.'

'For half a mile anyway.'

'Your eyes, that strange colour, they must be deers' eyes.'

'They're just brown.'

'When I held you yesterday I thought it was a deer I was holding. You struggled like one. I once rescued a deer that had got entangled in a fence. It was frantic to get away. Just like you, Effie.'

'I promise not to struggle so much next time.'

Then Morag came running up to them, red blotches on her face and roses in her hands.

'The midges are awful,' she gasped.

Effie and Hamilton hadn't noticed the voracious little beasts. They did now.

They all ran towards the house.

Twenty-four

HE WAS in his study, reading, when there was a timid knock on the door.

It was Effie. She had been upstairs putting the children to bed.

'I'm sorry if I'm disturbing you.'

He shut the book and stood up. 'I never mind being disturbed by you, Effie.'

'I'd like to ask a favour.'

'Anything, Effie.'

'Is it too late to take me to the Big Stone?'

'It's not too late. There are still two hours of daylight left. But,' – he went close to her and lowered his voice – 'it's a creepy place in the evening, with all the shadows, the kind of place where a beautiful girl who had once been a deer might be turned back into one.'

'I don't think I'd mind being a deer again, for a little while anyway.'

'I would mind it very much, if you suddenly made off for the high hills and were never seen again. What would I do then?'

'Become a deer yourself, perhaps?'

'But I don't have the magic, Effie.'

'How far is it to the Big Stone?'

'About a mile and a half.'

'Am I being a nuisance?'

'You could never be a nuisance. Shall we go by car or shall we walk?'

'I'd like to walk. It's a lovely evening.'

'I suggest putting dabs of oil of citronella on our noses and behind our ears, to keep off the midges. It's effective for about half an hour. There's some marshy ground to cross.'

'I'll take off my shoes. I often walk barefooted. My feet are tough. Like hooves.'

She was growing confident enough to poke fun at him.

It was a perfect evening as they walked along the road. They were alone in the world. No cars passed. There was no boat on the loch, no plane in the sky. The midges had not yet been alerted.

He took her hand. She withdrew it, gently. He did not know whether to be alarmed or delighted or both. He was in danger of becoming too fond of, no, of falling in love with, this strange girl who had come to him from nowhere.

'What did the doctor say in the note?' she asked. 'Or is it confidential?'

'He prescribed a month, two months would be better, of rest and recuperation in the Old Manse nursing home.'

'For Morag?'

'For you all.'

'There's nothing wrong with me.'

Why then had she had one of her fits of weeping last night?

'We can't stay as long as that.'

'Why not? I thought you were all happy here.'

'Too happy. Eddie says he'll run away and hide in the trees if we try to take him away.'

'It would be the death of Morag if she had to go back to sleeping in a tent.'

'Yes, but why should you have all the trouble and expense?'

'I don't mind.'

'You owe us nothing. You're a stranger.'

For a few minutes they were silent.

They came to the place where they had to climb a fence into the forest.

It was a high fence, with barbed wire. Care was needed. He offered to help her.

She laughed. 'I've climbed hundreds of fences.'

Even so she stumbled and might have fallen or got caught in the barbed wire if he hadn't caught her. As she had promised she didn't struggle this time, though he held her longer than was necessary. He felt her trembling.

'I think, Effie, I'm in love with you.'

'You hardly know me.'

She said it as a humorous reproof, but what she was feeling was great joy.

Even if it wasn't true – and how could it possibly be true? – she would remember him saying it all her life. God knew what was going to happen to her, but even if all her dreams faded and came to nothing and she ended up like those withered old women in Miss McDonald's pictures she would still feel proud that Gavin Hamilton, the kindest man she had ever known, who had helped her and her family more than anyone else ever had, had said he loved her.

'I'd like to spend the rest of my life getting to know you, Effie.'

It would take that long, he thought; there would be many discoveries.

What if she went away and he never saw her again? He must prevent that.

Trouserlegs rolled up, they pushed their way through a thicket of bog myrtle, bog cotton, stunted alder and birch. There were hundreds of marigolds.

Soon they came to a clearing. There was the Big Stone, deserving its name, as big as a house, as round as a ball, green with moss and grass, purple, red and white with lichen.

Anyone who hadn't known there were graves there would not have noticed the traces.

Effie stood looking down at them, as still as a deer.

Hamilton imagined the scene eighty years ago. A few tinkers, there to mourn but keeping out of the way. Three coffins, one small, all of the cheapest wood. No flowers. No minister. Mr Rutherford's grandfather wearing black gloves. The little boy, the survivor, bewildered. Had someone tried to console him?

That little boy, now an old man of eighty-four, was dying, murmuring poems he had spent his life composing. Surely some were about this sad burial ground.

He made up his mind. He went over to Effie.

She smiled eagerly at him. It was as if his being there was a comfort to her.

'They were my family,' she said.

'Mine too, Effie, if you'll let me.'

She didn't know what he meant.

'I've never asked about your family, Gavin. I'm sorry.'

'I don't have one. My parents died when I was a child. I have no brothers or sisters. So I have no family. Perhaps I have one now.'

'Morag and Eddie think you have.'

'What about you, Effie? What do you think?'

She still didn't know what he was getting at.

She teased him. 'Do you want me to be your sister?'

'No. My fiancée.'

She was astounded.

'I'd like to announce our engagement on Saturday as part of the birthday celebrations. That's to say, if you're willing.'

'Are you making fun of me?'

'I was never more in earnest. I want to have the right to look after you and the children; also, to chase off admirers like Hamish.'

He smiled. So did she.

What was happening? Something wonderful, but she wasn't sure what it was.

Again she teased him. 'Would it give you the right to sleep with me?'

'No, it would not. That could wait till we're married.'

Married? Was he seriously thinking of marrying her?

'It wouldn't stop you from becoming a minister, would it?'

'You'd help me to become one.'

Had he realised that in her own way she was as ambitious as himself? She would like very much to be a minister's wife. What could be more respectable?

She had noticed that he did not find it easy to get to know people. He kept too aloof. She had seen how awkward his workmates were when talking to him.

It was so different with children. He took to them immediately and they to him.

If he was to marry some superior lady like Miss McDonald he would become still more distant. He wouldn't laugh very often, either. How different if he was to marry Effie, the tinker girl, who knew what it was to be humble and who saw the funny side of things.

The midges had been massing for an attack. Now they launched it, in their thousands.

The effect of the citronella had worn off. He pulled up two fronds of bracken, one for her and one for him. They waved these frantically in front of their faces.

'Let's go home,' he said.

Home was a word she did not often use.

Twenty-five

HER MOTHER was feeling depressed and embittered. Either Daniel had been in an accident or, at his wife's funeral, he had met another woman, one with money.

She was in no mood to congratulate Effie.

'It's just a trick to get you into his bed. That's been his plan from the beginning. Do you think if you'd been flat-chested and squint-eyed he'd have invited you into his house? Once he's had you a few times and maybe got you bairned he'll throw you aside like used toilet paper. Remember Annie Gibson.'

Annie Gibson's story was still told on campsites, though it had happened more than fifty years ago. A well-to-do gentleman, and his lady wife, had come looking for a nice young girl, to look after their children. She had soon found she had other duties. She had to sleep with the master and any of his friends he wished to oblige. His wife didn't mind. That was what traveller girls were for. Annie became pregnant. She was at once got rid of. Her family refused to take her back. It was thought that she'd been given some money and packed off to Glasgow, where she became a prostitute.

Her story had been told as a warning to the discontented traveller girls.

'Gavin's not like that,' said Effie, 'and I'm not like Annie. He loves me. He's talked about marrying me.'

'God help you, girl, did you believe him?'

'Yes, I believe him.'

'Don't think that because he's going to be a preacher he's different. Look at the size of this house. It had to be big because the ministers that lived in it had such large families. They didn't get them by praying.'

'I know I could make him a good wife.'

'You could make any man a good wife, if you were left in peace to do it. But the world's full of bad-minded jealous bastards who would make it impossible.'

'He would help me.'

'My God, Effie, I believe you mean it.'

'Yes, I do mean it.'

'But does he?'

Effie laughed. 'I'll ask him.'

Before going to bed Effie, accompanied by Gavin, went out to make sure that the two old horses were comfortable. Maggie's leg was better; she no longer limped. Jess was thoroughly enjoying her long rest.

They showed their thanks by making a fuss of Effie.

She felt carefree and happy.

It was a beautiful night. The air was scented with roses.

She put her arm through his and took him on a stroll about the moonlit field.

'Do you know what my mother said about us? She said you just wanted to sleep with me.'

She found herself hoping that he would laugh and say, 'Well, why not?'

Instead, he said, rather peevishly, 'I hope you told her she was wrong.'

'She said that if I had been flat-chested and squint-eyed you wouldn't have given me a second look.'

He was somewhat crestfallen then, for of course there was a grain of truth in the accusation.

He was as easy to tease as Eddie. She felt protective. She would tease him but she wouldn't let anyone else do it.

'Am I to have a ring, to show that I'm engaged?'

'Yes, of course. We'll get one on Saturday.'

'But I need it tomorrow.'

He laughed. 'Why, what's happening tomorrow?'

'I want to go into town, by myself and walk among the people, your people, Gavin, as if I was one of them, because I will be one of them, won't I?'

He was amused but puzzled. There were times when she was too deep for him.

'I want to go into a hairdresser's and get my hair cut; it would be the first time in my life. I want to go into the hotel and order coffee. I want to go in and out of shops without being afraid of being suspected of shop-lifting. I want to stand among people on the pier, watching the steamer come in.'

Those things, which other women did every day, would be for her, new, terrifying experiences.

If her confidence faltered, as it was bound to do, and she could not bear to look or to be looked at, and she felt closer to the swans in the harbour than the people around her, she would look at the ring on her finger, and her confidence would be restored.

He thought, fondly, that she just wanted to show off her ring, as women did.

'I'd like to be there to see you marching into the Royal.'

'Oh, I won't march. I'll walk in elegantly.' And she would be trying not to look afraid.

Twenty-six

THE FIRST test would be the journey into town on Willie's bus. It came from further up the loch and probably would have passengers who had heard that Gavin Hamilton had allowed tinkers to camp in his field. They might not know yet that he had invited them into his house.

She had taken great care with her appearance. Morag had helped. It was Morag who arranged the white ribbon in her hair.

'Doesn't it make me look too young?' she had asked.

'But you are young, Effie. You're only twenty on Saturday. You're younger than Gavin.'

'Yes, I'm younger than him.'

'But he's not old.'

'No, he's not old.'

'He's not nearly as old as Daniel.'

'No.'

'Is Daniel coming here?'

'I think so.'

'Why is he coming?'

'To attend Grandfather's funeral.'

'Doesn't he want to marry you, Effie?'

That really was his purpose.

Effie could not help shuddering

'He's too old, Effie. Marry Gavin.'

'I'll think about it.'

They decided she should wear the red dress. It had been bought in a charity shop in Inverness, handed in by a titled lady. When new, it must have cost a great deal.

Effie usually did not wear a bra. She did not need one; her breasts were firm and strong. Today she put one on, making sure it did not emphasise her bosom too much or flatten it either.

'Will I do?' she asked.

'You're beautiful, Effie.'

'Not so beautiful as you will be some day.'

They hugged each other then.

She was waiting at the Old Manse gate when the bus appeared.

As she got on board she saw that there were other passengers, all women, all elderly, the kind who would be least tolerant and sympathetic.

'How are you today, Miss Williamson?' asked Willie, as she paid her fare.

'Fine, thank you.'

'Don't worry. I've told them you're a visitor from Inverness.'

Effie smiled at the other passengers as she took her seat.

'Good morning, ladies,' she said.

They were delighted with her. It never entered their heads that she might be a tinker.

'Has Gavin got rid of those tinker pests yet?' asked one.

'No, not yet.'

'He should get the police to them.'

While Effie, feeling guilty, was considering whether or not to be honest and tell them who she was another passenger whom she hadn't noticed spoke up, loudly complaining. This was a sheep tethered at the back. It kept it up all the way.

Willie always helped ladies off his bus.

'No need to look so worried, Miss Williamson,' he whispered. 'It's none of their business or anybody's but your own. May I say no handsomer young woman will be seen in Towellan today?'

'Thank you.'

'Will you be going back with me?'

'Yes.'

'Outside the Royal at four o'clock then. Good luck.'

He had guessed, quicker than Gavin, what her purpose was.

One Willie the Bus, she thought would make up for a hundred 'bad-minded jealous bastards'.

Twenty-seven

As SHE made her way to the jeweller's she wished, ruefully, that Gavin had not teased her about her being elegant. She felt self-conscious and a little silly. Then she caught sight of two swans in the harbour. She stopped to look at them and be comforted. How elegant in water their natural element, how clumsy on land. When she gave up the primitive travelling life it would not be all gain. She would lose this feeling of kinship with wild creatures.

Swans were faithful to each other all their lives. She hoped she and Gavin would be like that.

Some children were throwing pieces of bread into the air for gulls to catch in their beaks. The birds seemed to be enjoying the game as much as the children.

It was the kind of scene she had often watched, from a distance, not able to take part in it. Now she could, or rather when she had Gavin's ring on her finger, she could. It would represent her becoming one of his people.

Coming towards her was a young woman pushing a pram. The baby threw out a teddy bear. It too was playing a game.

Effie picked up the toy and returned it to the baby.

Into her mind came an incident that had happened a few years ago in a northern town. A little girl had taken Morag's hand. Immediately her mother, screaming, had rushed forward and dragged her away, as if Morag had been covered in scabs. Morag had never spoken about it but Effie was sure she remembered it often.

So would this young mother, protective of her child, repulse Effie in the same way? On the contrary, she was flattered and delighted that this mannerly, well-dressed young lady, no doubt a holidaymaker and probably staying at the hotel, was being gracious and helpful.

'A little girl?' asked Effie.

'Yes.'

'What's her name?'

'Donaldina.'

'After her father?'

'And her grandfather.'

Effie held the baby's tiny hand.

There was no horrified scream, no revulsion, the baby laughed happily. She had blue eyes.

'She's beautiful,' said Effie.

'We all think so.'

Effie was relieved to find Mr Lojko's shop empty.

He remembered her and greeted her warmly.

'The pearls have been much admired,' he said. 'Look.'

He pulled out a tray with half a dozen gold rings on it; each one had a pearl.

'Would they do for engagement rings?' asked Effie, shyly.

'Certainly.'

'I would like to buy one.'

'Take your pick. For you, young lady, a special price.'

'I haven't got money with me. Will it be all right if Gavin pays for it on Saturday? Gavin Hamilton, I mean.'

'Of course. I don't wish to be inquisitive, Miss Williamson, but am I to understand that you and Mr Hamilton have decided to become engaged?'

'Yes.'

'Congratulations. What a very nice thing to happen. I'm so pleased. You will be staying at Kilcalmonell then?'

'I think so.'

'He's a very lucky young man. I shall tell him so on Saturday.'

As she left the shop, with the ring on her finger, she felt that everything she saw was new, had just happened. It was as if everybody and everything had been given a fresh start.

She felt so confident that she decided to make the hair-dresser's her next call.

She went into the shop with her head held high, but her heart was sinking ever so little. It was not likely that the young women who worked in this place had heard about the tinkers who had come to Kilcalmonell. It wasn't the kind of thing they would be interested in. But what if they were suspicious and asked questions? What answers would she give?

On one score she did not have to feel embarrassed. Her head was clean. She had once been commended by a nurse who inspected campsites.

The three attendants, two of them as young as Effie herself, had elaborate coiffures that made her white ribbon look childish.

They stared at her with interest. She was a stranger.

'Could I make an appointment to have my hair cut?' she asked.

'You could have it done now if you like. We're not busy.'

'Thank you.'

The girl who was to attend to her was talkative.

'My name's Catriona.'

'Mine's Effie.'

'Short for Euphemia?'

'Yes.'

'Here on holiday?'

'Yes.'

'Staying at the hotel?'

'No.'

Effie could not resist boasting a little. She had had so few triumphs in her life that she could not forgo this, by far the sweetest.

'I'm staying at Kilcalmonell.'

'I didn't know there was a hotel there. Are you in a B&B?'

Effie did not know what a B&B was.

'I'm staying at the Old Manse.'

The scissors stopped clipping.

'But that's Gavin Hamilton's house.'

'Yes, I'm staying with Gavin.'

'You must know him well.'

'I'm engaged to him.'

She did not flaunt the ring but it was noticed.

'Did you hear that, girls? She's engaged to Gavin Hamilton. The sly monkey, he's never let on. Where are you from?'

'Inverness.'

'You're not local then?'

'No.'

'We've all got a crush on Gavin.'

'That cute beard!'

'Those blue eyes.'

'Those magnificent legs. You'll know he's a great football player?'

'Yes.'

Eddie was much impressed by Gavin's skill with a football.

Effie was not feeling as confident as she sounded.

She had not lied. She *was* engaged to Gavin. She *was* staying at his house. She did come from Inverness or near enough. Surely she was not obliged to tell them more than that?

Suppose she did tell them what would they do and say? Order her out of the shop? Immediately disinfect the comb and scissors?

But it was not a traveller or tinker who had come into their shop. That Effie Williamson was gone for good.

Perhaps she was being unfair to them. Perhaps, like Willie the Bus and Mr Lojko the jeweller, they would wish her well.

She gave a generous tip.

'Be sure to tell Gavin we were asking for him,' said Catriona.

It was now time for morning coffee. She had to screw up her courage again. At the hotel entrance she almost hurried past. She was afraid it was going to be too much for her.

She looked at the ring.

Resolutely and elegantly she walked in.

No one in the coffee room looked surprised to see her. One man gave her an admiring glance.

The waitress smiled. 'Black or white?' she asked.

Effie's usual drink was tea in a smoky billy-can.

'White, please.'

'Would you like anything to eat? Biscuits?'

'Yes, please.'

When the waitress went to the kitchen with the order she remarked it was for a very nice young lady. 'A real beauty. Wearing a dress that must have cost a small fortune.'

When she came back with the coffee and biscuits she couldn't resist chatting. She liked the way the young lady spoke.

'Are you here on holiday?'

'Yes.'

'You're lucky with the weather.'

'Yes.'

'There's not a nicer place than Towellan when the sun shines.'

'It's a beautiful little town. The people are very friendly.'

'Have you visited the old castle? Robert the Bruce stayed there, or so they say.'

Effie had never heard of Robert the Bruce.

'Him who beat the English at Bannockburn. When was that again? 1314. That's a date every Scots schoolchild knows. You'll find a brochure on the table in the foyer that tells you all about it. There's a fine view of the town from the castle.'

'Thank you.'

Again Effie left a generous tip. She had begun to feel very nervous.

Though she had done well and no one could have suspected that she was playing a part she was assailed by cold black doubts as she stepped into the bright warm street.

She was finding it easy to deceive people. Gavin had been the easiest. But she could not deceive herself. Her high opinion of herself was not justified. She was ignorant. She did not know things that schoolchildren and middle-aged waitresses did. She could read but only if the words were simple and even then very slowly. She could hardly claim to be able to write. Gavin had made no attempt to find out how poorly educated she was, and she had made the feeblest attempt to tell him.

She tried to convince herself that if she worked hard and was given help she could remedy those shortcomings, and so she could, but it would take a long time, years perhaps.

Really it was ridiculous for her to think that she could ever marry a man like Gavin Hamilton.

You've got yourself into an awful mess this time, Effie, she told herself. You've turned your back on travelling and pearl-fishing, and you've just discovered that to be accepted as one of Gavin's people you'd have to keep on pretending, and you couldn't possibly keep it up, you'd give yourself away sooner or later.

She had left herself and the children with nowhere to go.

She had tried very hard to keep Morag and Eddie with her, but it looked now as if she had failed. They would have to be put in a home, where it wouldn't matter whether they were wanted or not, whether they were loved or not. No one wanted them. Their mother didn't; she saw them as evidence of her own failure and disappointment. Daniel Stewart didn't, though it was possible he was Morag's father. If he had shown genuine affection for them and had been willing to take them to live with him, he could have had Effie as a reward.

All right, Effie, face up to it. You'll have to return to Sutherland, to travelling and pearl-fishing. You'll have to agree to the children being put into a home, for a little while anyway. How long, though, was a little while? Six months? A year? Five years? Perhaps the home would be close enough for her to be able to visit them, once or twice a year at least.

She would have to forget that such a place as the Old Manse, Kilcalmonell, ever existed.

She would weep but she had learned long ago that there had to be an end to weeping.

She would never marry and would never have children of her own. Would one of those children who would never now exist have had Gavin's blue eyes?

She took off the ring and put it in her pocket.

At the pier a crowd of people were waiting for the steamer. It could be seen in the distance, with its red and black funnels and its escort of clamorous gulls.

The women were in their summer dresses, the men in flannels and open-necked shirts. One old man wore a Panama hat. Strangers talked to one another. A tight hold was kept on toddlers. Faces were sunburnt. A band played.

Effie was given more than her share of smiles. Some had admiration in them, all had goodwill.

They did not know she was an impostor.

When the steamer had come and gone, and the pier was deserted she decided to pass some time by visiting the old castle.

As she went up the steep path she met a family coming down. There was a girl, a little older than Morag, with a big dog on a lead. It was called Rex.

It growled at Effie. She thought, rather bitterly, that she might deceive people but not dogs. It smelled the traveller in her.

She patted it on its head.

Immediately its growl changed to a friendly bark.

'That girl,' said the little boy, 'isn't afraid of dogs.'

In her mind she heard Eddie crying, 'Effie isn't afraid of anything.'

Thanks, Eddie, but I'm afraid of lots of things.

As she wandered among the ruins it struck her that the lords and ladies who had lived there hundreds of years ago must have had to suffer some of the hardships that travellers did today. They had no bathrooms for instance, no flush toilets, no toilet paper, no showers, and no electricity.

She sat on a bench painstakingly reading what it said in the brochure about the castle and other places of interest. Kilcalmonell was mentioned and the Old Manse. It said that the Old Manse was soon to be taken over by Glasgow Council to be used as a holiday home for city children.

Effie felt a great longing to be a part of that holiday home. She would scrub floors, make beds, wash dishes, peel potatoes, and want no wages if only the children and she were allowed to stay there, in safety.

Gavin would be at college in Glasgow. But she mustn't think of him.

After lunch in a café, not the hotel, she would hire a boat and row out to the swans. She would ask their advice.

Twenty-eight

'Give Gavin my regards,' said Willie, 'and mind, if you need a change, you're welcome anytime. There's plenty of room.'

'Thank you.'

Morag and Eddie were waiting for her at the gate. She was especially glad to see them after being among so many strangers.

Eddie did not notice the anxiety in her smile, but Morag did.

'Did anything happen, Effie?' she asked.

She meant, were you insulted, jeered at, made to feel cheap and worthless?

'No, pet. Everybody was very nice.'

Because she had succeeded in deceiving them.

They went up the drive to the house.

'Daniel's come,' said Eddie, resentfully. 'Me and Morag hid in the bracken.'

'His caravan's very nice,' said Morag.

'Did you go in it?'

'No. Mother took him up to see Grandfather, but Grandfather was sleeping. Is there anything wrong, Effie?'

Effie could not truthfully say there was nothing wrong.

'It's because Daniel's come,' said Eddie. 'He wants to marry Effie. Well, he can't because she's going to marry Mr Hamilton. What did you bring me, Effie?'

'A toy motor car.'

'Is it the kind that winds up?'

'I think so.'

'What colour is it?'

'Red.'

'Good. What did you bring Morag?'

'A little doll.'

'You shouldn't have brought us anything,' said Morag, sternly. 'We need all our money for food.'

'Mr Hamilton's got lots of money.'

'We can't ask Mr Hamilton for money. Can we, Effie?'

'Why can't we? He's going to marry Effie. Then his money will be hers too. That's what being married means, doesn't it, Effie?'

There was no one at the caravan. Effie decided to put off going to greet Daniel.

'I'm going upstairs to change my dress. Will you come with me, Morag? Eddie can stay downstairs and play with his car.'

'You just want to tell her something without me,' said Eddie, 'but I don't care.'

Effie felt guilty. The cheap presents were poor compensation for their having to leave this comfortable house where they felt so happy and safe.

Morag sat on the bed watching Effie take off her dress and hang it up in the wardrobe. She did not notice Effie making sure the ring was still in the pocket.

Effie put on the slacks and white blouse that Mrs McTeague had given her.

'Gavin likes you better in a dress,' said Morag.

'Does he? How do you know?'

'I can tell. He's always looking at you. What is it you want to say to me, Effie?'

Effie sat on the bed and put her arm round Morag's neck.

'How do you know, you little witch, that I want to say something to you?'

'I know you, Effie.'

'I want your advice, Morag. I asked two swans for their advice. I want to know if you agree with them.'

Morag smiled. 'Did they speak to you?'

'They didn't have to.'

'I'm only ten and I'm not clever, but I'll tell you what I think.'

'You know we're travellers. That's what people call us because we move about from place to place. Some people call us tinkers but we don't mend pots and pans.'

'Tinkers move about too, Effie.'

'And they sleep in tents like us. We're often dirty and smelly. We can't help it because we have to wash ourselves in cold burns. When I was your age I was ordered out of a school because the mothers of the other children said I gave them nits and lice. So I did. We're called trash. We're not allowed to camp near houses. People throw stones at us. They get their dogs to chase us away. We're terribly poor.'

'Why are you telling me all this, Effie? I know it.'

'It's what I should have said to the people I met today. I wasn't brave enough.'

'You didn't have to tell them anything, Effie. It was none of their business.'

'But I wanted to be one of them. I wanted them to respect me.'

Morag wasn't convinced. 'Was this what you wanted to talk to me about?'

'I wanted to tell you that we're leaving the day after tomorrow.'

'Leaving here? Leaving this house? Leaving Gavin?'

'Yes, pet. We've been here long enough. It's not fair to Mr Hamilton.'

'He's not Mr Hamilton. He's Gavin. Did he say we have to leave?'

'He's too kind, too polite, ever to say it. People will be saying bad things about him. They'll be saying how can he become a minister if he lets a trashy tinker girl live in his house.'

'You're not a trashy tinker girl.'

'That's what they'll think I am. The ladies in his church. The men who work with him. Everybody he knows.'

'But you don't sleep with him, Effie.'

Effie blinked. This was her ten-year-old sister speaking.

'If you were older, Morag, you'd understand.'

'I'm old enough. Have you told him we're leaving?'

'I'm going to tell him when he comes home from work.'

'You can tell him, Effie. I won't. Where will we go?'

'Willie the bus driver said we could camp at his place for as long as we liked. It's not far.'

'After that where will we go?'

'I thought we'd go to Inverness. I know people there. They could find me a job.'

'What about me and Eddie? Will we have to go into a home?'

'Maybe for a little while.'

'That's what you said last time, Effie. We were in for nearly a year.'

'I promise it won't be as long this time.'

'How do you know? You've got no money. And who's

going to tell Eddie? He'll run away. Why shouldn't Eddie and me stay here with Gavin. We don't have to go with you, if we don't want to. I can cook. I can make beds. I can scrub floors.'

'But I don't want us to be separated. When families break up it's not easy for them to get together again.'

'It's you that's breaking us up, Effie. If Eddie and me have to go into a home I'll never speak to you again.'

Morag then got off the bed and rushed out of the room.

Effie had never felt more miserable and useless. All the many doors between her and happiness, and her family's happiness, were shut and locked.

She went downstairs to help prepare the evening meal but she did not stay to share it. She had no appetite and had a headache.

Eddie was sympathetic and suggested she should take an aspirin.

Morag would not speak to her. It couldn't be dismissed as a childish huff. She was being deserted by someone she loved and had trusted.

Eddie had not yet been told. He was happy and carefree playing with his new toy.

Morag had put her doll back into its box. It was a symbol of her sister's treachery.

Effie went upstairs and cried.

She hated feeling sorry for herself but she could not help it. She was too young to have all these responsibilities. Many girls her age were still at college.

In the camps they all said how capable she was. She had saved a child from drowning. She had beaten off a savage dog. She had faced up to officious policemen. She had confronted farmers trying to cheat her and her friends out of what they had earned.

She had no close friend in whom to confide. She had had one but Shona had died of consumption, aged eighteen.

She must not give in. She got up and went into the bathroom to wipe away all traces of tears. She put on a little lipstick.

She stared at herself in the mirror.

'Who are you?' she asked, contemptuously. 'You're not Effie Williamson. She doesn't cry when things go wrong.'

She would not tell Gavin that they were leaving. They would steal away when he was at work.

She said by the window, waiting for him to come home.

She heard him putting his bicycle in the shed at the gate.

Eddie must have gone down to meet him. She heard them talking and laughing. Eddie would be showing him the toy car.

He always had a shower and change of clothes before he ate. He was pernickety about cleanliness. He would have had an awful time as a traveller.

She smiled but was close to tears again.

At last he was coming up the stairs. Her heart was beating very fast.

He knocked on the door, quietly, as if he thought she might be asleep.

'Come in,' she called.

She had decided to speak humorously.

He came in. 'Eddie said you were not feeling well.'

Eddie, not Morag. Morag still hadn't forgiven her. Perhaps she never would.

He went over and put his hand on her shoulder.

'Well, how did you get on? Did you find what you were looking for?'

'Was I looking for something?'

He laughed. 'I got that impression. Your hair's very nice.'

'The girls in the shop send you their regards. They seemed to know you.'

'Well, I occasionally have my hair trimmed. Did you buy a ring?'

'I told Mr Lojko you'd pay for it on Saturday.'

'You're not wearing it. Are you saving it for Saturday?'

Suddenly she changed her mind. She must tell him that they were leaving. Sneaking off without telling him would be cowardly and dishonourable. She would feel ashamed all her life.

She tried to speak light-heartedly, as if what she was saying was no more than a casual by the way.

'I've got something to tell you. We're leaving the day after tomorrow. We can't leave tomorrow, there are too many things to see to. It's not fair to you, us being here, me being here. Miss McDonald was shocked. They all will be.'

He said nothing.

'We'll go to Willie's place. He said we could stay as long as we liked. So we'll stay till after the funeral. Then I think we'll go to Inverness. I know people there. They'll find me a job. If not I'll go back to pearl-fishing for a little while. I might be lucky and find a lot of valuable pearls. The children may have to go into a home. It wouldn't be for long. I don't want us to be separated but it can't be helped.'

She managed to stop. It wasn't like her to babble on, self-pityingly.

He still said nothing. He must be relieved but was too polite to say so.

'Is that how you see the future, Effie?'

She nodded.

'It's not quite how I see it.'

She pretended to be interested in a yacht out on the loch. She wasn't going to listen to him. What was between them, whatever it had been, was gone.

'First of all, you're not going anywhere. You're my future, you and the children. We'll announce our engagement on Saturday. Hugh McTeague and Sheila have agreed to be our witnesses. After that we'll be able to get married in four weeks, when the banns have been called. I'm assuming you have no objection to being married in church. If you have we'll be married in any way you please.

'You know that this house is going to be used as a holiday home for children. I was asked if I could find suitable staff locally. You would be perfect for the job, Effie.'

'Wouldn't they want someone better educated?'

'Children like you, Effie. Besides, as my wife you'd have a better right than anyone. You and the children would live in the house.'

'Where would you live?'

'Here too, with you. I expect I'd be at university in Glasgow, but I'd come home at the weekends. Sometimes you could bring the children to visit me in Glasgow.'

It was too much for her. All those doors between her and happiness were unlocked and thrown wide open. She burst into tears.

He was reassuring her when Morag came in. She had come to make her peace with her sister.

Twenty-nine

HAMILTON TOOK her hand as they were about to cross the field to the caravan.

She was trembling. 'We don't have to go in.'

'Are you afraid of him?'

'No, but he'll remind me of things I'd rather forget.'

'Would you like me to go and tell him you're not ready to see him yet?'

'I'll be all right if you're with me. He'll say things that aren't true. He'll say I promised to marry him. I was just fifteen at the time. I didn't. They all wanted me to marry him. It was for my own good, they said. He gave my grandfather money. I never felt safe.'

'Dear Effie, you're safe now.'

'I hope you believe me, Gavin, when I tell you he never touched me. No man's ever touched me, in that way. I used to sleep with a knife under my pillow.'

'Good God! Of course I believe you.'

'Shall we go and get it over with?'

Hand in hand they approached the caravan.

'He likes gaudy colours,' said Hamilton.

'He's quite a peacock.'

A curtain was drawn aside. A face peered out.

'He'll be very interested in you, Gavin.'

She knocked on the door.

Her mother opened it, looking flustered. Two buttons on her blouse were unfastened. Her skirt was on back to front. She was drunk, amiably so.

'Would you like to come in? It's worth seeing. He's got it up like a bridal chamber. He meant it for you, Effie, but he's having to make do with me instead.'

Effie was shaking her head. She did not want to go in.

'If you don't mind, Mrs Williamson,' said Hamilton, 'we'll stay outside. Effie's not been so well today.'

Daniel appeared then, showing a mouthful of bad teeth set in a diffident, ingratiating leer. He was drunk too.

His hair was white, his nose purple, his cheeks bright red.

His pale-blue trousers were held up by an ornate belt, his pink shirt was caught in his trouser zip.

His speech was slurred.

'Hello, Effie. You're looking marvellous. Isn't she looking marvellous, Nellie?'

Mrs Williamson adjusted his zip.

'This is Mr Hamilton, who's been so kind to us.'

'Nellie's been telling me about you, Mr Hamilton. What she didn't say and what I want to know is what a man like you wants with a little traveller lass like my wee Effie.'

'She's not wee,' said Mrs Williamson, 'and she's not yours.'

'I've known her all her life. I nursed her on my lap when she was a baby. How long have you known her, Mr Hamilton? Hardly a week. I hope you've not been taking liberties with her. I hope you've not been harrying her sweet little nest.'

He began to sob.

'They're getting married, Daniel. Just like you and me. Tell you what, Effie, if you and Mr Hamilton come to our wedding Daniel and me will come to yours.'

Effie looked aghast, but Hamilton enthusiastically agreed. 'Where will you be married, Mrs Williamson?'

'At Dalnessie, in Sutherland. It's a favourite campsite for travellers. Hundreds will come. Daniel's well-known and Grandfather's a patriarch.'

'It would be an opportunity for me to meet some of Effie's old friends.'

'It would and they'd make you very welcome.'

Effie was not looking quite so aghast.

She was realising that he could have chosen no more convincing way of showing that his interest in her, and that his affection for her and her family was sincere.

Daniel had fallen asleep on his feet.

'Would you be so kind, Mr Hamilton, as to help me get him back to bed?'

Hamilton picked him up and carried him in.

The pillows had red hearts on them.

When he came out Mrs Williamson had a surprise for him. She gave him a hug. 'You're a good man, Gavin Hamilton. I hope Effie knows how lucky she is.'

So lucky indeed that she couldn't yet believe it.

'We'd better go and see what the children are up to. We'll see you later, mother.'

On their way back to the house Hamilton put his arm round her. 'I'm sorry, Effie. I should have consulted you first.'

'Yes.' But she was glad he hadn't. She wouldn't have known what to say.

'A mother should be present at her daughter's wedding, and a daughter should be present at her mother's. Don't you agree?'

'Were you serious about meeting some of my old friends?'

'Very serious. Everyone who was kind to you, Effie, I want to meet and thank them.'

'Even those in Miss McDonald's pictures?'

'Why not?'

'Why not! You're like a child at times, Gavin.'

It was meant as praise, though spoken with a little exasperation.

'I take that as a compliment. Children are much nicer than adults.'

She would have to admit that.

'Sometimes, Effie, one has to make a fool of oneself.'

She did not quite understand. 'You didn't make a fool of yourself. My mother doesn't think so anyway. You've made her very happy.'

If she was ever to introduce him to her friends among the travellers, especially girls her own age, she would probably feel a little embarrassed but she would also feel very proud. He would be as gentlemanly towards them as if they were titled ladies. He would have no condescension. They would be charmed. They would envy her.

Thirty

THAT NIGHT, after the children were asleep Effie and Gavin sat side by side on the sofa in the big room, discussing their immediate future.

Effie did most of the talking.

'I want you to help me improve my reading and writing. I'd like to learn to drive the car. We'll have to enrol Morag and Eddie in the local school. We'll keep old Maggie for Morag and Eddie. We could offer the horse to the McTeagues. Deirdre would like that. We'll burn the tents and get rid of the carts.'

She looked up and caught him gazing at her with fond amusement.

'If I'm talking too much just tell me to shut up. I'm a blether when I get started.'

This was a girl whose long silences had worried him.

He felt a great desire to protect her. She was so eager, so naive, so hopeful, so brave, so young, so vulnerable. Cruel forces had been stalking her all her life. Now that she was almost out of their reach they would be most determined.

'Tell me, Gavin, what are the duties of a minister's wife?'

He had yet to learn that in her own way she was as ambitious as himself. For years she had had to endure humiliations that had threatened to stifle her spirit, and she had often dreamed of reaching a position where one day she would be free of them.

Now, through Gavin Hamilton, had her chance come? By helping him to achieve his ambition she could achieve her own. If he became a minister, respected by everyone, as his wife she would be respected too.

He had come to appreciate her irony and counter it with his own.

'Well, if she's amenable she helps him in his church business.'

'What's amenable?'

'Willing to do what she's asked to do without grumbling.'

'Aren't all ministers' wives amenable?'

'I'm afraid not all.'

'Why do they marry ministers then?'

'Because they love them, I suppose. You see, some of them have careers of their own.'

'What kind of careers?'

'Schoolteachers. Civil servants. Lawyers even.'

'But not pearl-fishers?'

'You'd be the first, Effie.'

'The amenable ones, what do they have to do?'

'They don't *have* to do anything. If they want to help that's up to them. If they don't that's up to them too.'

'Those that want to help, what do they do?'

'Well, they go to church on Sunday mornings.'

'What if they have small children to look after?'

'I expect they'll employ a babysitter.'

'What else?'

'They join in the hymn-singing.'

'I could do that. I'm quite a good singer. I might not understand the words but I'm sure I would like the tunes.'

'They help to decorate the church with flowers.'

'I'd like doing that.'

'They visit the sick and elderly.'

'I could do that.'

'If there's a Bible class they might be expected to take part.'

'I'm not sure about that. I don't know the Bible very well. But I could learn.'

'I'm sure you could.'

'Do you think I'd make a good minister's wife?'

'People would flock to my church just to see my beautiful wife.'

'What if the minister's wife has a different religion to him?'

'Are you hinting that you're a Buddhist?'

'Gavin, a university professor said that travellers were pagans. What's a pagan?'

'I believe it's someone with no religion.'

'Then I'm not a pagan. I have a religion. I'll tell you about it when I know you better.'

She stood up. 'Would you like a cup of tea before going to bed?'

'That would be very nice.'

'Shall I bring it in here or shall we go to the kitchen?'

'Let's go to the kitchen.'

So, minutes later, they were in the kitchen drinking tea and nibbling biscuits.

'If anything happened to me,' she said, 'would you take care of the children?'

He caught a glimpse of those cruel forces.

'Nothing's going to happen to you.'

'No, but if something did?'

'You know I would, Effie.'

They went up the stairs together.

'I'll sit with your grandfather for a little while.'

'He won't know you're there.'

'I'm not so sure. Anyway, you go to bed. You've had a tiring day. Good night.'

She made to go into her room, very quietly, so as not to disturb Morag, but turned. She was going to say something but didn't. 'Good night, Gavin.'

She would find it easy to get to sleep. There had been nights, many of them, when she had lain awake for hours, tormented by fears and worries. It was wonderful to feel relaxed and safe like this.

Morag murmured in her sleep. It was a contented sigh. Previously it would have been a moan or even the terrified cry of a nightmare.

Thirty-one

EFFIE AND Morag sat in the back, Eddie in front with Hamilton.

'We're just like a family,' whispered Morag.

'We are a family.'

'You know what I mean.'

'Yes, pet, I know.'

Effie was afraid that they might meet some of Gavin's workmates or friends, especially the big man who had called her trash. He could hardly do so this afternoon for, with Morag's help, she had made the best of her appearance. Even Eddie complimented her. 'You look great, Effie.' No one would recognise her as the ragamuffin who had arrived last Saturday on a cart, dirty and smelly. In the red dress and yellow cardigan, with the necklace of blue stones, she was a different person altogether. Where, though, had that dirty smelly creature gone?

As they stood at the seafront, waiting for the McTeagues, they were given friendly greetings, or at least Hamilton was. He was well-known and well-liked. Effie herself got curious looks.

He came and stood beside her, close enough to touch. He made no attempt to hide his feelings for her. He kept smiling at her, fondly and proudly.

She, though, could not get it out of her head that she was an impostor. This handsome girl in the red dress didn't exist. The real Effie Williamson was skulking in a tent somewhere, alone and miserable, with nothing to look forward to.

Thirty-two

IN THE car on the way to Towellan the McTeagues discussed her. Mrs McTeague wasn't sure that they were doing the right thing by encouraging the engagement. It was too soon. It could result in disaster for them both, especially for poor Effie. To be ruthlessly frank, what was she, after all, in spite of her pride and beauty? Member of an outcast tribe, with primitive habits and customs. She was keeping up a pretence and was doing it bravely, but she couldn't hope to keep it up forever.

'You're wrong, mother,' said Deirdre. 'They'll get married and be very happy.'

'I'm sure we all hope so, dear.'

'Why Gavin is in such a hurry,' said Mr McTeague, 'is that he doesn't want someone like Hamish McKenzie to sneak in and carry her off.'

Ian had no opinion on the subject. 'I wonder if Eddie's seen more otters.'

When the McTeagues arrived Deirdre was out of the car first. She ran over to Effie and hugged her.

'She really is a splendid girl,' whispered Mrs McTeague.

Her husband chuckled. 'Gavin knows what he's doing.'

Eddie wanted to know if it was time to go along to the cinema. If they didn't hurry there would be no seats left.

He was almost right. The film was a very popular one, especially with children, so the cinema was packed. They could not get seats together. Eddie insisted on sitting beside Hamilton.

'He may get very excited,' said Effie. 'Maybe I should sit beside him.'

'He's fine with me.'

In the film there was a sequence in which the two comedians were trying to deliver a big piano up a long flight of steep stairs. With prodigious efforts they would manage to get it almost to the top when it would slide back down, almost crushing them under it. The children were greatly amused but the more sensitive ones were alarmed too. None was more affected than Eddie who went into fits of hysterical laughter mixed with tears. A couple seated near him looked at one another.

Luckily there was another film about a small boy who had lost his collie. It turned up safely in the end and Eddie was greatly relieved.

When they came out of the cinema Deirdre took charge.

The grown-ups were to go for a walk while the children went to the souvenir shop and bought birthday presents for Effie. They all had money.

It gave Hamilton an opportunity to slip into the jeweller's.

Effie had a quiet word with Eddie and Morag. 'Keep an eye on him in the shop, Morag. Eddie, don't touch anything you're not going to buy. No stealing. Mr Hamilton would be very angry.'

Eddie promised solemnly.

The four children rushed off to the shop.

At the hotel they were given a small private room. The waitress who had served Effie coffee and given her a history lesson attended them. She had been told it was a birthday celebration. She did not yet know it was also to celebrate an engagement, and she was far from knowing that the tall black-haired girl in the red dress, and her little brother and sister, had been, as recently as last week, travellers, or tinkers as they were called locally. Indeed, in the kitchen she had surmised that Effie must belong to one of the upper-class well-to-do Argyll families who lived in big houses up lonely glens or beside remote lochs. She had the presence and the dignity of such a girl. What she noticeably lacked was the haughtiness.

Hamilton was well known in the town. Though he was only a forestry worker it was generally believed that, once he became a minister, he would be a man of importance. The Old Manse with its rose garden was one of the finest houses in the county, situated in one of the most beautiful spots.

Deirdre was still in charge. Only Eddie dared to question her authority and he was easily won over by her letting him sit where he pleased and giving him first choice of paper hats. He chose a silver crown.

Hamilton sat next to Effie. This was not as Deirdre had planned it, but he insisted and she had to humour him. After all he would have to be close to Effie if he was to put the ring on her finger.

When it came to the giving of the presents Eddie clamoured to be first. His offering was a tartan ball-point pen. 'You said you were going to write letters, Effie.'

Ian's present was a china otter. 'You could put it on your mantelpiece.'

Morag had chosen a brooch in the shape of a thistle.

Deirdre's present was a small china doll with blue eyes, dressed in McTeague tartan. 'You could give it to your own little girl, Effie, when you have one.'

Mr and Mrs McTeague gave a box of handkerchiefs. Effie would have been embarrassed if they had bought her something more costly.

Then it was Hamilton's turn. They watched him expectantly.

Effie was on the verge of tears but she still managed to exchange a secret smile with Morag.

He took out of his pocket a small rectangular box covered with blue velvet. He handed it to Effie. 'Happy birthday, Effie. Many happy returns.'

'Open it, Effie,' cried Eddie.

She opened it. Revealed was a small elegant expensive wristwatch. 'Thank you, Gavin,' she whispered.

'Put it on, Effie,' cried Eddie.

Effie put it on. They all admired it. Deirdre made sure it was set at the right time.

Now came the most important part.

Nobody was going to make a speech.

'Have you got the ring, Gavin?' asked Deirdre.

He produced it out of another little box.

It was golden, with a Scottish pearl mounted on it.

Without waiting for Deirdre's cue he took hold of Effie's left hand and slipped it on the requisite finger.

'This is for always, Effie.'

'For always, Gavin.'

He kissed her.

Mr and Mrs McTeague offered their congratulations. Mrs McTeague was in tears. 'I hope it's a success.'

'What's to stop it?'

But Hugh was always optimistic. He would order trees to be planted in places where others were sure they wouldn't grow. He was usually right too.

Thirty-three

As soon as she got home Effie went to the caravan to show her ring and watch to her mother.

Her mother wasn't drunk but she wasn't cheerful either. She and Daniel had had another of their disagreements.

'It's not the ring that matters, Effie. It's the promise it stands for.'

'I know that, mother.'

'Rings aren't easily broken. Promises are.'

'Not Gavin's.'

'No man's to be trusted, Effie.'

'He is.'

'I hope so. I've got a present for you too, Effie. Well, Daniel and I have. Just a minute.'

She came out with a flat white box. It contained, wrapped in pink tissue paper, two silk scarves.

'He brought two, one for you and one for me. He said he remembered how you liked the feel of silk against your skin.'

'How is he?'

'He says it's his stomach but he's really sick with disappointment and jealousy.'

It wasn't in Effie's nature to be ungracious and revengeful. She would never wear the scarf, it would be too intimate a reminder of a man who had once tried to rape her, but she would take it and give it to Morag when he was gone.

'Thank him for me.'

'Come in and thank him yourself.'

'Later.'

'Not too much later. He's talking about leaving on Monday. He can't afford to wait any longer.'

'Will you be going with him?'

'That's still to be settled. But I think I will.'

'You'll miss Grandfather's funeral.'

'That wouldn't break my heart. You'll have Hamilton to stand by you. He won't be jealous about the scarf. He's not small-minded.'

I'm the one that's small-minded, thought Effie.

She went off to join Hamilton, Morag, and Eddie. Eddie was organising a race.

'What was that about?' asked Hamilton.

'I'll tell you later.'

She couldn't resist, though, pressing her face against his breast. This was now her sanctuary.

He felt her shivering. He stroked her head.

Eddie watched, impatiently. He was about to start the race and here was Effie still holding things back. Morag watched too and was glad for Effie. It was silly of her, just ten, being jealous of Effie, yet she was, a little.

Eddie got them lined up, giving himself a very generous start. He suspected that Hamilton would not try as hard as he should to beat Effie. He had noticed, and been reasonably pleased, that Hamilton would give Effie everything he had, but he ought to do his best to beat her. What was the use of a race if everybody didn't try to win?

Never had Effie been so light-footed and light-hearted.

She ran, Hamilton said, like a deer. He kept close behind her and at the finish where they arrived together caught her in his arms.

Eddie came up, puffing. He declared Effie the winner but claimed that he would have won if he hadn't slid over.

In the caravan, looking out of the window, Mrs Williamson was proud of her daughter.

'She's beautiful, but what's better she's happy. Come and look.'

Daniel dragged himself to the window. 'She's happy all right but she'll pay for it.'

'What do you mean? She's already paid for it, all her life.'

'I'm remembering when old Bella read her palm. She wouldn't tell us what she saw in it. It must have been something terrible.'

'She was a drunk old fraud.'

'She was often right, Nellie.'

'She was often wrong.'

'But there have been other signs.'

'Signs of what?'

'Signs that she could have a great misfortune in front of her.'

'Are you hoping she does?'

'God forgive you, Nellie. I wish her nothing but good.'

'You're rotten with jealousy.'

'I would give every penny I have to save her from whatever it is.'

'Liar.'

'Look what happened to her grandmother, your mother, Nellie.'

'God forgive you for bringing that up.'

'It happened, Nellie.'

'My mother was married to a man who had little respect for her and not much affection. Effie's going to be married to a man that's very fond of her and admires her immensely. There's no comparison.'

Thirty-four

THAT NIGHT, when Effie and Hamilton were having their cup of tea before going to bed – it was going to be a nightly habit of theirs – Hamilton startled her by saying, 'Would you like to come to church with me tomorrow?'

She had thought about asking him to take her but had decided it was too soon. She wasn't ready herself yet and the ladies with the hats had to be given more time to get used to the idea of a tinker girl being engaged to, and likely to marry, someone highly respected in the community. Some of them were bound to disapprove. From their point of view Effie was a brazen, unscrupulous, designing young adventuress, using her lucky good looks to seduce a man whose reckless and sometimes simple-minded desire to show himself a good Christian made him susceptible. They would honestly believe that she would mean ruin for him. Had she not thought so herself?

Her hand was on the table, the left one with the ring. He put his hand over it. 'Does it take all that thought?' He laughed. 'They'll be fascinated by you. They've never met anyone like you before.'

'Not all of them.'

'Most of them.'

'Not Miss McDonald and her friends.'

'You'll never forgive her, will you, Effie?'

She was indignant. She withdrew her hand. 'If you think I have a grudge against her for showing you those pictures you're wrong. She wasn't trying to hurt me. I didn't matter, she was trying to save you.'

He put his hand back. 'You keep surprising me, Effie Williamson.'

'It would be the second time I've been in a church.'

'When was the first time?'

'Years ago, when I was ten. It was in Inverness.'

Where the churches were substantial and the congregations solidly respectable.

'The door was open. It was a hot day. I suppose I was wearing a ragged dress, not too clean. Lots of well-dressed ladies wearing hats. One, with a kind face, came up to me and said I was in the wrong place. She took me to the door. They were all staring.'

'Poor Effie!'

'I wasn't being impudent. I was just curious. I wanted to know how other people lived. I wanted to learn.'

She was quite excited.

'It would be very different tomorrow.'

She smiled. 'I'll be properly dressed. I'll try to look as if I had a right to be there. But I'll not say anything to anybody. Will you sit beside me?'

'Won't I want to show off my beautiful fiancée?'

'No, you mustn't do that.'

Suddenly he realised what an ordeal it would be for her.

'Perhaps it's not such a good idea, Effie. Let's wait till another Sunday.'

'But I have to know if I'm doing right. Mrs McTeague doesn't think so. She didn't say it but I could tell.'

'In what way doing right?'

'In becoming engaged to you, in letting you talk about us getting married.'

'But, Effie, I thought that was settled.'

'I have to be very sure.'

'Are you saying that if a few narrow-minded silly women are unpleasant to you you'll give me back my ring?'

'They might not be narrow-minded and silly. They might be sensible and wish me well. They'll just think that if you marry me it will be a terrible mistake.'

'Effie Williamson, I'm going to ask you just one question. Do *you* believe that if you married me it would damage my career as a minister? Look at me, Effie.'

She looked at him. She spoke quietly. 'No, I don't.'

Thirty-five

MORAG WAS watching Effie getting dressed for church. Hamilton had already left to pick up the ladies in their distant glen. He would come back soon for Effie.

Morag would never have admitted it, she would have died first, but she was hoping, well, was letting a tiny hope enter her mind, that Effie would not go to the church.

She had become afraid that Effie was growing further and further way from her and Eddie. At the church she would meet people whom Morag and Eddie would never be able to meet.

Here was Effie singing happily and yet she must surely know that Morag was worried. It seemed as if she didn't care.

Morag could not resist saying, 'The people you'll meet in the church, Effie, will they know you're backward, like me and Eddie?'

Effie turned to stare in astonishment. 'What do you mean?'

'Well, you *are* backward, Effie, aren't you? I can read quicker than you and everybody knows I'm backward.'

'Why are you saying this, Morag?'

Effie felt devastated. She wanted to creep into a corner and weep. Here was her most loyal, most loving ally, turned against her, so cruelly, so unfairly.

'Don't you want me to do well, Morag? For all our sakes? Don't you want me to marry Gavin so that we'll have a home of our own, you, me, Eddie, and Gavin?'

'Maybe Gavin will meet somebody else, somebody that's been to college. That could happen, couldn't it?'

'Yes, it could.'

Effie went over and sat beside her sister.

'Do you want to go back to sleeping in a tent for the rest of your life?'

'No.'

'You like it here, don't you?'

'Yes.'

'Then you've got to help me.'

'How can I help you, Effie? I'm only ten.'

'Just love me. Just be on my side. Just help me not to feel frightened.'

'Do you feel frightened, Effie?'

She didn't have to ask. More than once she had heard Effie weeping in the night.

'Are you frightened for Eddie and me?'

'Yes, pet, and for myself too.'

'But Gavin wouldn't let anything happen to you.'

There were things, though, nameless things, which even Gavin couldn't help.

Still, it was a great comfort to be able to depend on him.

At the church she would do her best to make him proud of her.

Thirty-six

ON SUNNY Sunday mornings the congregation of Kilcalmonell Parish Church, a small select company, liked to arrive early so that they could enjoy a chat in the kirk-yard overlooking the loch, among the six ancient yews and seventeenth-century tombstones. It was a beautiful peaceful place where it felt pleasant to be alive and where it would be a privilege to be buried. However, those well-to-do middle-class matrons who made up the majority never gave a thought to the historic bones under their shoes. They were much more interested in the gossip, decorously exchanged.

On that particular Sunday there was an unusually large turnout and an air of anticipation among them, hardly to be attributed to their looking forward to Mr McDonald's sermon which, as always, would be worthy but uninspired. No, what was causing the excitement was that someone, no one was quite sure who, had started a rumour that Gavin Hamilton had got himself engaged to the tinker girl who was living in his house and was bringing her to the kirk that morning.

It was the kind of quixotic gesture he was fond of making. Another example had been his giving of his unopened pay packet to a passing tramp.

Those who carefully measured their own charity thought

he had a damned cheek trying to show himself more Christian than anyone else.

This exploitation of the unfortunate girl was the kind of thing that would appeal to him. The dirtier, smellier, stupider she was, the better for his purpose.

Nevertheless their arrival was eagerly awaited.

Whenever a car arrived those with a good view of the car park would shake their heads at those who hadn't.

It was, one woman said, oblivious to the irony, a bit like waiting for royalty.

Then the headshakings became vigorous nods, followed immediately by gestures of surprise and disappointment.

It was soon seen why. Coming through the gate, arm-in-arm, were Hamilton and a girl, no, a young lady, who was no tinker slut. In a black outfit, bareheaded, with hair magnificently dark, she carried herself with enviable grace. She looked a little shy but quite composed.

It was just like Gavin, champion of the poor and the despised, to have found for himself a fiancée whose family evidently had money and distinction. It was never forgotten that old Mrs Latimer had more or less made him her heir.

They were all keen to be introduced to the girl but there were too many of them and besides it was time to proceed into the church, where Miss Fiona had been playing the organ for the past ten minutes.

Miss Fiona looked up and saw them. She of course recognised the girl as the tinker, but she could not very well stand up and, as it were, unmask the impostor.

It wasn't she therefore who did the unmasking. It could have been someone who had seen the girl on Willie's bus. Whoever it was, it spread through the small church until almost everyone knew.

There was silent consternation. What was to be done? They had greeted this scruffy girl as if she was a person of consequence. But really she could hardly be called scruffy. Indeed they had thought her beautiful and they still had to think of her as beautiful, she hadn't changed all that much in the past few minutes. How to remedy their mistake without looking foolish? Hamilton had played a trick on them. They could hardly apologise. It needed one of them, one with authority to sort things out on behalf of all of them. There was Muriel Gilmour, but she was unpredictable.

Though a stalwart Tory she was no snob. She was capable of seeing a person's worth however lowly that person's status.

When the kirk was skailing Mrs Gilmour pursued Hamilton and his girlfriend.

'Just a minute, Gavin. Aren't you going to introduce me?'

'With pleasure.' He introduced them.

'Congratulations to you both.'

Those listening wondered if Muriel had understood. She was sometimes not that quick on the uptake.

'Bring her along to Rhubaan one of these days. I'd like a chat with her.'

Mrs Gilmour then went off to the car park where her friends were waiting. 'I don't give a damn what she is or what she's been, she's got character. I like her.'

Thirty-seven

THAT SUNDAY evening Morag went upstairs to go to the bathroom and look in on her grandfather. She thought he was dead and ran downstairs to tell Effie and Hamilton.

They were in the big room. He was helping her to improve her reading.

Effie had noticed that Morag hadn't yet asked her how she had got on at the church.

Effie and Hamilton hurried upstairs.

Effie was still feeling a certain pleasure after her triumph that morning. She kept holding on to Hamilton.

The old man wasn't dead but was very close to it.

'If we're going to give him his wish to die in a tent we should take him down now.'

'He doesn't know where he is, Gavin.'

'Still, we promised.'

'I promised. You didn't.'

'Your promise is my promise, Effie.'

Their shared experience in the church had brought them closer. They knew each other better.

'Will we wait for my mother and Daniel?'

'No need. We'll manage. The bed's ready, isn't it?'

'Yes.'

Hamilton had no difficulty picking up the frail old man,

carrying him downstairs, and laying him on the bed where Effie made him as comfortable as she could.

She felt strange seeing Hamilton in the tent with her.

'I'll not miss him. That's a terrible thing to say, but it's true. He tried to *sell* me once. He didn't want me to get away. He wanted me to pay for what he did to my grandmother.'

'If it hadn't been for him, Effie, I would never have met you.'

They stood outside the tent. He had his arm round her. Her body was still unfamiliar to him.

'I'll wait here for a while,' she said.

'No, you go and rest.'

He felt a great desire, a great need, to protect her, but from what? Her enemies were memories, not easily got rid of.

Morag came slowly up to them. It seemed to Hamilton there was menace in the little girl's manner, but surely that was ridiculous.

He noticed, though, that she smiled at him but would not look at Effie.

'Where's Eddie?' he asked.

'Hiding.'

'Hiding? Why is he hiding? Who is he hiding from?'

'Effie.'

'Is it some kind of game?'

'I told him she wants to put us, me and him, in a home.'

'That's silly,' said Effie, weakly.

'You said it, Effie.'

'Yes, but it's different now. I didn't know what we were going to do.'

'What's this about?' asked Hamilton.

'It's something she's got into her mind.'

'You put it in my mind, Effie.'

Effie burst into tears and ran towards the house.

'You've upset her, Morag. I won't let anyone upset Effie.'

'It's not my fault she's weepy. She cries in her sleep.'

He remembered the doctor's warning.

'Wait here for your mother and Daniel,' he said. 'I want to talk to Effie.'

He found her in the big room with the book they had been reading open on her lap.

He sat beside her. He took out his handkerchief and wiped her tears.

'You've got to let me make a fuss of you, Effie.'

'I did tell her that she and Eddie might have to go into a home.'

'But that was when you didn't know what else to do. She's confused, Effie.'

'It's not her fault.'

'She said something that alarmed me. She said you often cry in your sleep.'

'Not often, I hope. My mother used to say that since I never cried when I was awake I made up for it by crying in my sleep.'

'It's not a joke, Effie.'

'No, it's not a joke.'

'Why, Effie, why?' But it was very stupid of him to ask why.

'You helped to cause it, Gavin.'

'Me?'

'I used to dream of someone, some kind man, like you, who would come and take me away and marry me. Not on a white horse, an old blue car would have done. You never came.'

'I've come now.'

'I'm still not sure you're real.'

She touched his cheek.

'Do you know what else she said? She said that if I slept with you you wouldn't cry.'

'Well, I wouldn't want to wake you, would I? Do you want to sleep with me, Gavin?'

'Very much, after we're married. That's what we agreed, wasn't it?'

She seemed to hesitate. 'Yes.'

'I've been thinking that we ought to invite Mrs Gilmour to the wedding.'

Effie was laughing a little when they heard a loud wailing outside.

'Your mother, Effie. Your grandfather must be dead.'

Tearing her hair, as well as wailing, Mrs Williamson rushed in, with Daniel behind her.

'He's gone, Effie. Do you know, Mr Hamilton, if people knew hundreds would come to the funeral. He was a famous man among his own people.'

'We could put a notice in the local Tain newspaper, with an account of the funeral.'

'I'd appreciate that very much.'

Daniel sighed. 'There will be lots of expenses, Effie. You'll have used up all your pearls.'

'I've still got some left.'

'Keep them as souvenirs,' said Hamilton. 'I'll take care of the arrangements; you and I together, Effie.'

'One thing I can be sure of, Effie,' said her mother, 'when I leave I won't have to worry about you and the kids. I'd like to thank you again, Mr Hamilton.'

Effie was staring in wonder at Hamilton. He would do

anything to oblige not just her, but her mother too; he was even friendly to Daniel. Yet he was still a stranger.

Surely he must have doubts. In putting off their sleeping together was he avoiding that commitment and so giving himself time and opportunity to change his mind?

She would not blame him.

As for herself she had not yet got rid of a guilty feeling, not that she was not worthy of him but that she had no right to love him or be loved by him.

Thirty-eight

MR RUTHERFORD, undertaker, was waiting in his office for Miss Effie Williamson, tinker girl, so that he could tell her of the arrangements he had made for the burial of her grandfather at the Big Stone.

She would be accompanied by Gavin Hamilton, in whose house she was at present staying. Their relationship was not quite clear. That they were engaged to be married, as was rumoured, Mr Rutherford just could not believe, though he wished them both well. As far as he knew Hamilton was too ambitious and self-sufficient to saddle himself with a girl who, however personable, was dirt poor, uneducated, used to living in tents, and, to be indelicate, used to lavatories that were the outdoors.

Nevertheless it seemed that at Kilcalmonell Kirk on Sunday she had caused quite a sensation.

But all that was none of Mr Rutherford's business. His business was to carry out this unusual interment with style and efficiency, and to expect a fair price; which was why he welcomed the involvement of Hamilton, who could afford to pay.

Mr Rutherford had reason to be pleased with himself. He had good news for Miss Williamson.

To begin with, to his own surprise he had been granted permission for the burial by the Forestry Commission.

The plain truth was – to be kept from Miss Williamson –

no one wanted the old man's remains. Mr Rutherford had applied tentatively to four local kirks and had been given unChristian rebuffs. The authorities who managed Towellan cemetery had been very sweirt. Superstition seemed to have contributed to their unwillingness, but the reason they had given, in ashamed mumbles, was that since the old man seemed to have been a patriarch of sorts among the tinker community there would be frequent pilgrimages to his grave, and the last thing Towellan wanted was the invasion of those pitiable but undesirable nomads.

The Big Stone was out of everybody's sight and it would give the old man his dying wish to be buried beside his family. For that reason his granddaughter, this Miss Williamson, had, rather heroically, brought him all the way from Sutherland, a distance of over two hundred miles.

The police had had to be consulted. Here was another surprise. Mr Rutherford had expected pig-headed opposition from them, but no, perhaps because of secret orders from their superiors, they cooperated willingly, with the meek suggestion that there should be as little publicity as possible. They pointed out it was a single track road to the Big Stone and they didn't want it jammed with sightseers' cars and the passing places illegally used as car parks.

Mr Rutherford was not sure whether to pray for a sunny day, which would mean a goodly crowd or a misty drizzly day which might reduce the attendance but would give an appropriately mournful atmosphere.

Mr Rutherford expected at least fifty to attend. Locals were curious and holidaymakers were always on the lookout for free entertainment.

He was interrupted in his reverie by the sound of a car stopping outside and the slamming of car doors.

Soon there was a knock on the door and in came Hamilton and the girl, she looking very young in a simple brown dress white at the collar and cuffs.

Mr Rutherford had instantly to revise his opinion as to their relationship or at any rate Hamilton's to her. He gave the impression that if asked to choose between one day occupying the pulpit in St Giles' in Edinburgh, that Church of Scotland pinnacle, or marrying this girl he would without hesitation have chosen her. But being the kind of man he was he would want both and might well get them.

Mr Rutherford had too casually dismissed the girl as personable. He now saw she was much more than that, she had a natural grace astonishing in someone with her background.

Mr Rutherford had been wondering what kind of religious service she would want, if indeed she wanted any. He had no idea what the religious beliefs of travellers or tinkers were. It was true that Miss Williamson had been to church on Sunday but that surely had been to please Hamilton. If they ever got married it would probably be in a church, but again it would be to please Hamilton.

As for Hamilton he was a Christian, an over-zealous one at that, but like other ambitious young men entering the Church of Scotland ministry nowadays he had no patience with impossibilities like the Resurrection, the Virgin Birth, and other miracles. He saw Jesus Christ as a Great Example, which seemed to Mr Rutherford as rational an attitude as any.

'Do you wish a short service, Miss Williamson?' Mr Rutherford used his softest voice. He liked this girl.

'My grandfather didn't want one. He wanted me to say a poem.'

'One of his own? I understand he was a poet.'

'Yes.'

'Gaelic?'

'Yes.'

'Its subject no doubt the sad events of eighty years ago?'

'Yes. Gavin will explain first. Then I'll say the poem.'

Hamilton looked at her anxiously. She was very calm now but how would she be, in that place of poignant memories, with people watching and curlews calling, as they had done all those years ago?

Not for the first time Mr Rutherford regretted not knowing Gaelic, that ancient and noble language.

'Is Mr McTeague supplying bearers?' asked Hamilton.

'Four men have volunteered.'

'Do you know their names?'

'I believe Mr McDougall, the foreman, is one. I understand he insisted.'

'You see, Effie,' whispered Hamilton.

They got up to go.

'By the way, Miss Williamson,' said Mr Rutherford, 'would your grandfather have liked a piper, playing a lament or two?'

'I think he would. He played the pipes himself when he was younger.'

At Highland games, no doubt, but more likely as a beggar than a competitor.

Hamilton and Effie drove round to the harbour and sat in the car.

The nearest fishing boat was called Aphrodite.

Hamilton smiled. 'A good omen, Effie. Who'd have thought a fishing boat in Towellan would be called Aphrodite?'

'What does it mean?'

'Aphrodite was the Greek goddess of love. She rose up out of the sea.'

'I wish I knew as much as you do, Gavin.'

'One day you'll know more.'

'The foreman, Gavin, he was the one who said I was trash.'

'Yes, but I'm sure he's sorry now.'

'You were angry with him.'

'Very angry. So was Hugh McTeague. Some of the others weren't pleased either. Perhaps he's trying to make amends.'

'He could call me trash if he liked but not the children. They're not to blame.'

They sat in silence.

'What time is it?'

She glanced at her watch. 'Just leaving half past eleven.'

'Let's go for a walk about the town and then have lunch in the Royal.'

He noticed her smile but not the faint shiver that went with it.

Going for a walk about the town and then having lunch in the Royal for him and most people were ordinary everyday things, but for her they were still ordeals calling for resolution and a little defiance, with despair only a little way off.

She must be patient. It would take time. He would help her.

There was a great danger, though, that she might end up belonging nowhere.

Thirty-nine

SHEILA MCTEAGUE wasn't able to be at the funeral, having to stay at home to look after her own two children and Morag and Eddie.

On Thursday, at half-past two, while she knew the funeral would be in progress, her telephone rang.

It was Fiona McDonald. Her voice was almost unrecognisable. It kept rising to hysteria.

'I'm glad, Sheila, you're not at that awful funeral.'

'Aren't all funerals awful, in the true sense of the word? Don't we Christians believe that God is present at every death?'

That stumped Fiona for half a minute at least.

'I meant disgusting.'

Sheila hadn't realised how insanely and how unhappily jealous Fiona must be. She felt almost sorry for her.

'That tinker bitch has got her claws into Gavin. *She's* disgusting.'

'That's the last word I would have used to describe her. She's delightful.'

'We'll have to get rid of her and send her back to the filthy dumps she came from. For Gavin's sake. She's bewitched him with her pretty face and big breasts.'

Big breasts? Mrs McTeague, tempted to be bitchy herself, reflected that Fiona was flat-chested.

'I wouldn't call her pretty. She's got too much character in her face. As for her breasts I would say she's got a fine womanly figure.'

'She mustn't be allowed to marry him. It would ruin him. We've got to stop it.'

'How can we stop it if that's what they want? Why should we want to stop it? They love each other.'

'Don't be ridiculous. He's only known her for a week. How can he possibly love her?'

He had known Fiona for several years. 'It happens, Fiona.'

'What do her kind know about love? They're no better than animals.'

'I think she's a sensitive, intelligent young woman. If you bully her and try to drive her away Gavin would never speak to you again. Neither would I. She's done wonderfully, with help from no one. She'd make him a good wife.'

Weeping hysterically, Miss Fiona then screamed words that as a minister's sister and a minister's daughter she ought not to have known, far less used.

Forty

MR RUTHERFORD had guessed, optimistically, that there might be as many as thirty spectators. The people who would attend could hardly be called mourners. It turned out that there were more than double that number. Their cars lined the road for half a mile, and occupied all the passing places, to the annoyance of the two constables on traffic duty. Thank God, they grumbled, it would be over in less than an hour.

The fence had been temporarily removed so that those who didn't mind getting their feet wet were able to venture over the wet carpet of marigolds and bog myrtle to the Big Stone, where they were rewarded with an unrestricted view of the proceedings. Those who remained on the road, dryshod, had their view obscured by the screen of stunted birches and alders, but they were able to hear everything.

It was generally agreed that the girl in the black costume, the old man's granddaughter, was the star turn. Everyone was impressed by her composure, remarkable in someone so young, and, most of all, by a quality they couldn't help being aware of but couldn't quite give a name to. In the midst of all those people she looked as if she was on her own. Even the young man with the beard, who looked like a superior sort of tinker, was excluded, though he had announced himself to be her fiancée. He kept close to her, though, and once or twice touched her shoulder.

There were some who saw her as a wild creature, say, on the alert all the time, ready to bound off up through the trees to the hilltops, where she would feel more at home than in any house.

She spoke the poem in a clear, steady, resolute voice. Though it was in Gaelic, the native tongue of that part of the world, it might have been in Chinese for all that most of them made of it. It had been previously explained to them that it was about a family who had been buried in that same place eighty years ago.

When she was finished, quite a number, with tears in their eyes, went up to her to shake her hand and offer her condolences and congratulations.

'Are you all right, Effie?' whispered Hamilton.

'Yes, thank you, Gavin.'

But he could see how disturbed she was. He would have liked to take her in his arms and comfort her, but he was afraid she would repulse him, gently but firmly.

Hamilton had seen to it that Mrs Williamson and Daniel were given places close to the grave. She wept most of the time, he held his hat in his hand.

'God knows where she got it from,' sobbed Mrs Williamson, amazed at her daughter's calm competence. 'It wasn't from me and it wasn't from her father.'

That young ploughmen had been curly-haired and good-natured, but hardly bright.

'It's a fucking mystery, Nellie.'

'For God's sake, Watch your language. This is a funeral.'

'Sorry, Nellie, I'm still thinking of what big Bella said when she read Effie's palm.'

'Effie was just a bairn.'

'Our futures are in our hands, Nellie, from the day we're born.'

'You're still jealous.'

'I admit it. I've a right to be jealous. She was promised to me. What does he know about travellers?'

'That shows how stupid you are, Daniel. She sees him as her chance to be finished with travelling, with sleeping in tents and wandering all over the country on bumpy carts. Look at her. She's got it in her to be a lady.'

'What happens when he wants rid of her?'

'He's promised to marry her. He's given her a ring to prove it.'

'A ring's nothing. It's as easy to take it back as to give it. She'll end up wanted by nobody, with nowhere to go. Maybe that's what Bella saw in her hand.'

'You'd like that, Daniel. You would like her to have to come begging to you.'

'I wouldn't want her then.'

'Well, shut up. She's going to speak.'

Everybody had gone quiet. Effie was about to recite the poem.

When it was all over Hamilton and Effie took Mrs Williamson and Daniel back to the caravan. They had been included in the invitation to a meal in the McTeagues' house but had declined. Daniel was impatient to get on his way. He did not like driving in the dark.

The farewells were said at the caravan.

Mrs Williamson took Hamilton aside.

'Will you write and tell me how you're all getting on?'

'I promise. Remember Effie and I are going to your wedding and you and Daniel are coming to ours.'

She grinned. It would never happen but it pleased her to think that it might.

'I'd like to meet some of Effie's friends.'

He had said it before. He must mean it. He loved Effie, not just as she was now but as she had always been.

Despite what Daniel had said Mrs Williamson knew the danger wasn't that Hamilton might want to get rid of Effie, but that she might decide she had no right to love him, less marry him. If she got it into her head that her presence was doing him harm she would be off, even if she had no place to be off to. Also, let her think for a minute that he was sorry for her and that would be the end of it.

'Look after her, Gavin.'

It was the first time she had used his Christian name.

'You can depend on it.'

'She's not as sure of herself as she makes out.'

She had a last word with Effie.

'You'll not be sorry to see us go, love.'

'I hope you and Daniel are very happy, mother.'

'We'll never be as happy as you and Gavin, but we'll manage. Please, Effie.' She put her hand on Effie's arm. 'Don't spoil it for both of you.'

Effie smiled. It was not an easy smile to understand.

'I know you, Effie. You've got that thrawn bit in you. He loves you, anybody can see that. Don't, for Christ's sake, punish him for it. Be good to him. He needs you as much as you need him.'

'Haven't I got more reason to love him than he has to love me?'

It was said humorously but it worried Mrs Williamson.

It was as well that Hamilton wasn't the kind of man who would want a docile biddable wife who'd never contradict or tease him.

'Thanks again for taking care of the children.'

'It's Gavin you should thank for that.'

'I know. I've thanked him. He still talks about going to my wedding and meeting some of your old friends. I don't suppose he means it but it's very nice of him to say it.'

'He means it.'

'You won't try to stop him?'

'Why should I try to stop him?'

'I thought once you got away from travelling folk you'd never want to see them again.'

'I'm not ashamed of my friends.'

'You never were, love. I've asked him to look after you, Effie, now I'm asking you to look after him. Remember when we first met him. We couldn't understand him. He was too kind, too simple, too easily taken in. Look how he invited us to use his house. We could have been a gang of thieves.'

'I think I understand him a little better now.'

Then Daniel called anxiously. 'Time we got going, Nellie. It looks as if it's coming on to rain.'

'He doesn't like driving in the rain,' said Mrs Williamson.

Daniel helped her to climb aboard the caravan and then rather shakily followed her. He turned and gave Effie a wave. Reluctantly he included Hamilton in it.

Then the caravan was on its way.

Effie and Hamilton stood looking at each other.

'So, Miss Effie Williamson, that's the end of your travelling life.'

'I've lost some good friends.'

'Why should you lose them? You know where they are. We can visit them whenever you like.'

She smiled. 'We'll see.'

Forty-one

SHEILA AND Hugh McTeague were at their kitchen window, looking out for Effie and Hamilton. The children were in the living room, Deirdre and Morag playing with dolls, and Ian trying to teach Eddie the rules of chess.

Hugh was anxious. The rain was still heavy. All the burns would be overflowing, the roads would be flooded in places. Trees might have been blown down. There were flashes of lightning.

Sheila was anxious too but for a very different reason. In spite of what she had said so boldly to Fiona McDonald she still had doubts about Effie and Gavin. Though she had been careful, or hoped she had, not to encourage them too much she felt some responsibility for she had done nothing to dissuade them from their engagement. On the contrary, against her better judgment she had agreed to be a witness at the announcement. If something was to be done it would have to be done soon. Gavin's future was at risk. He had been their friend for years. Effie they hardly knew.

'I'm going to say something that might shock you, Hugh. It shocks me just to think it. But I think it should be said.'

He grinned. 'What is it?'

'Wouldn't Gavin be better off with Fiona?'

'Better off? What do you mean? He doesn't need her money.'

'I'm not talking about money. You know how ambitious he is. He's not going to be any ordinary minister. He's going to be famous. He's not going to be minister of a small parish like Kilcalmonell. His church is going to be one of the biggest ones in Glasgow or Edinburgh. Isn't that what he's told us?'

'Yes.'

'Wouldn't Fiona be a great help to him? She's got lots of influential Church connections. Her uncle was Moderator. She's a university graduate.

'We like Effie. We admire her. We wish her well. But she's quite uneducated. I'm sure she can hardly read or write. She's been a tinker all her life, and if her mother's an example she's got connections that would be disastrous for him.'

Hugh said nothing. He was shaking his head, though.

'Is it too late?'

'Too late for what?'

'To prevent it. To convince them it would be an awful mistake for them both. To convince her anyway.'

'But I don't think it would be an awful mistake. It would be if he married Fiona.'

'Are you so sure? Fiona's got a kind side to her nature if she would only show it oftener. She's well liked by the ladies of the church. She's in love with Gavin and has been for years. She might well bloom if she married him.'

'I don't want to say anything against the woman, but Gavin will never marry her. For one thing, she doesn't like children and he does. For another thing he's completely in love with Effie.'

'I sometimes think he's just sorry for her.'

'If she thought he was just sorry for her she'd be off. You know how proud she is.'

'Yes, and it's a bit silly. What's she got to be proud about?'

'A great deal. I thought you liked her. You said you thought she'd make him a good wife.'

Before Sheila could find an answer to that the car appeared out of the mist and rain.

Sheila and Hugh were at the door to greet their visitors.

Hamilton had his arm round Effie. They were laughing at the sheer malevolence of the wind that buffeted them and the rain that soaked them.

Sheila kissed Effie on the cheek. She did not think she was being hypocritical.

'Hugh said you did very well at the Big Stone. So calm. So brave.'

'She was marvellous,' said Hamilton.

'I was terrified,' said Effie.

Then Deirdre and Morag rushed up to Effie to show her their dolls.

In the hubbub Sheila snatched an opportunity to have a quick word with Effie.

'We saw the caravan going past about half an hour ago.'

'Didn't it stop?'

'No. You'll miss your mother.'

'Yes.'

'Did you never think of going back with her?'

'No. Do you think I should?'

It was a justified rebuke. Sheila felt ashamed but was still determined to save Gavin from this unsuitable young woman.

Her chance came when they were all at the table.

Deirdre wanted Effie to show them her engagement ring. Shyly, Effie held up her left hand.

'A handome girl like you, Effie, must have had lots of admirers,' said Sheila.

She ignored Hugh's shake of the head and Gavin's frown.

'Lots of men wanted Effie,' said Morag, 'but they didn't want me and Eddie.'

'Effie kept a knife under her pillow in the tent,' said Eddie.

'Good heavens, why?'

'A man came into the tent once and tried to tear off her clothes. He was drunk.'

Sheila thought there must have been many such unsavoury episodes in Effie's past. No doubt they accounted for the traces of coarseness in her face.

'Farmer Mitchell said he would take us, me and Eddie, if Effie would go with him. He had a big farm.'

'How would you have liked being a farmer's wife?' asked Sheila, laughing.

'He didn't want to marry me. He was over sixty.'

'Still, you must have seriously considered his offer, for the children's sake.'

'Yes.'

'I don't think Effie's enjoying this conversation,' said Hamilton.

He was jealous of a man he had never seen and would never meet.

It would not be easy to make him see sense where Effie was concerned. Even if Sheila had been able to tell him something very much to her discredit, such as that she had had a child by someone like Farmer Mitchell, he would still have wanted her.

Later, when Sheila and Effie were in the kitchen washing and drying the dishes Effie herself brought up the subject.

'You don't think Gavin should marry me, do you, Sheila?'

'Well, to tell the truth, Effie, I'm inclined to think it could be a big mistake, for both of you.'

Effie wasn't huffy or sulky, but she wasn't humble either.

'I can see why you might think it a mistake for Gavin, but how could it be for me? I would have a home, for the first time in my life; so would the children. I would have a husband who loved me and would take care of me and the children. How could that be a mistake?'

Sheila was disconcerted. She had not expected irony.

'If he was content to be a forestry worker all his life, Effie, it would be different. You would suit him well then. But he wants to become a minister. I don't mean any disrespect, Effie, but you have to admit that if he married you he would have to give it up. He would be terribly disappointed.'

'I don't have to admit that at all. Marrying me wouldn't stop him from becoming a minister. He says I could help him, and so I would. We've talked about it. I'm only just twenty. I've got plenty of time to learn what I need to learn.'

Sheila was again astonished. Somehow she had no difficulty in imagining this young woman in ten years' time, confident, and accomplished, fit to be the wife of any minister, however big his church.

There was a knock on the door. It was Gavin, looking for Effie.

'Effie, Hugh and I think we ought to be leaving soon, before the road's impassable.'

'You can stay the night here if you like,' said Sheila.

'Thanks, Sheila, but I think we would all like to go home. What do you say, Effie?'

Effie could have said that she had made longer journeys in worse weather on an open cart drawn by an exhausted pony. What she did say, quietly, was, 'You're the driver, Gavin. It's up to you.'

'But you think we should try?'

'Yes. We can always turn back.'

Ten minutes later, as Sheila, under an umbrella, stood in the doorway watching them get into the car she felt touched when Morag, clasping the doll Deirdre had given her, told Eddie he was to sit in the back with her. The seat in the front beside Gavin was for Effie. That was how families travelled.

The car set off into the storm.

'Will they make it, Hugh?'

'I think so. Gavin's a capable driver and he doesn't panic. Besides, he's got Effie with him. She'll back him up.'

Because Hamilton kept calm and cheerful, showing no sign of being afraid or losing his temper, all the others, including Effie, were able to look on the journey as an adventure.

In her quiet unassertive way Effie was a considerable help. She kept reassuring the children. Without being asked she got out and helped Hamilton to drag out of the way a fallen tree. With her skirts held up she waded into a flooded part to see how deep it was; it came above her knees. When at last they reached the Old Manse gate she got out and opened it, though the wind blowing off the loch was at its fiercest and branches of trees thrashed above her head. She was soaked when she came back into the car.

At last they were safely home, greatly relieved and pleased with themselves.

'Well done, Gavin,' said Effie. 'Didn't Gavin do well, children?'

Eddie had been frightened. 'Gavin's a good driver,' he shouted. 'I'm going to be a good driver when I grow up.'

'Don't boast,' said Morag, but she kissed him as she said it.

When they were all in the kitchen Effie hurried off to the bathroom for towels. Then she busied herself making them all comfortable. She put on the kettle, saying they could all do with a cup of hot tea.

Hamilton looked fondly on those maternal and wifely ministrations.

She noticed and was embarrassed. It was all right for her to be motherly but premature for her to be wifely.

They sat and sipped the tea, chatting about the visit to the McTeagues and the journey home.

Hamilton was concerned about the effect the experience might have on Morag's cough.

'I've coughed only three times today,' she said. 'The medicine you brought has done me good.'

This was how it would be, thought Effie, if Gavin and I were married; no, she should say when they were married. Sheila would be proved wrong.

Afterwards, at Hamilton's suggestion, they held a ceilidh in the big room, where the velvet curtains were drawn and a peat fire burned in the grate.

Effie played her accordion, Hamilton his fiddle, and Eddie his mouth organ though parts of it were missing. With her doll clasped in her arms Morag danced a sedate little dance, while singing a sedate little Gaelic lullaby.

At Eddie's request they played several games of snakes-and-ladders and ludo.

Effie asked Gavin to teach her how to play chess.

Twice Effie went to the back door and looked out on the storm.

*   *   *

Later when the children were asleep Effie and Gavin chatted in the kitchen.

'They've never been happier in their lives,' said Effie. 'Thanks to you.'

'No, Effie, most of the credit belongs to you. You've looked after them heroically.'

'I think I was about to give up.'

'Effie Williamson giving up? I don't believe it.'

'Effie Williamson's no heroine. I think we should have a serious talk, Gavin.'

'About what Sheila said to you? What did she say to you anyway?'

'She asked if I'd thought of going back with my mother.'

'That was none of her business.'

'She seems to have changed her mind about me. She thinks now that I'm not suitable.'

'Suitable for what?'

'Suitable to be married to you.'

'Mrs Gilmour and the ladies in the church thought you were suitable. So did the people at the Big Stone today.'

'I've always been good at pretending.'

'You weren't pretending. They saw the real Effie Williamson. My Effie Williamson.'

'But, Gavin, I'm not sure myself that I'm suitable.'

'You're not already married, are you?'

'Of course not.'

'Not even to Farmer Mitchell?'

'Especially not to Farmer Mitchell.'

'I'm not married either, especially not to Fiona McDonald. I love *you*, Effie.'

He waited for her to say it and she said it, quietly but earnestly.

'I love you, Gavin.'

'So we'll get married.'

'Is it as simple as that?'

'It is.'

They listened then in silence to the roaring of the wind in the big beech trees.

It was his turn to tease her. 'What did you think of Eddie's suggestion?'

'Which one? He's always making suggestions.'

'That you and I should sleep together.'

'He meant just sleep.'

She had thought about it. She had imagined it happening. With Daniel or Farmer Mitchell it would have been an agony and degradation. With Gavin Hamilton it would be a liberating, uplifting joy. It would really be making love.

'When we're married, Effie.'

'Yes, Gavin, when we're married.'

But would it ever happen? Would any of it happen?

In a few weeks would she really cease to be Effie Williamson, pearl-fisher, and become Mrs Gavin Hamilton, accepted and respected in the community? Would she go on living in this fine big house, with Morag and Eddie, and Gavin at weekends, looking after the children from Glasgow? Would she, able to drive by then, meet him in Towellan and bring him home? Would she, having worked very hard, no longer uneducated and ignorant, be able to help him achieve his ambitions, whatever they were? Would she decorate his church with flowers and on his behalf visit the sick? Would there be three children, one with brown eyes and two with blue? Would she and Gavin visit her old traveller friends?

Going up the stairs she paused and asked those questions.

In her room she stood in front of the mirror. It was still Effie Williamson who looked back at her, it was Effie Williamson who was to answer.

For a minute or so there was a tumult in her mind, like the storm outside, and then a great calm.

'Yes,' she murmured, 'yes, yes, yes.'

It could all happen.